BABY DRAMA II
(BABY DRAMA SERIES, BOOK 2)

SANDI LYNN

BABY DRAMA II

(Baby Drama Series, Book 2)

New York Times, USA Today & Wall Street Journal
Bestselling Author
SANDI LYNN

BABY DRAMA II
Copyright © 2024 Sandi Lynn Romance, LLC

All rights reserved. No part of this publication may be reproduced, distributed, or transmitted in any form or by any means, including photocopying, recording, or other electronic or mechanical methods, without the publisher's prior written permission.
This is a work of fiction. Names, characters, places, and incidents are the products of the author's imagination or are used fictitiously. Any resemblance to actual events, locales, or persons, living or dead, is entirely coincidental.

MISSION STATEMENT

Sandi Lynn Romance

Providing readers with romance novels that will whisk them away
to another world and from the daily grind of life – one book at a time.

CHAPTER 1

Stella

I stepped off the elevator and into the Park Avenue penthouse, which I visited daily, five days a week, Monday through Friday, with an occasional Saturday.

"Thank God you're here," Mrs. Kensington said as she strolled by me in her designer suit and Louboutin heels. "Austin is out of control this morning, and Jenna won't get out of bed."

"Morning, Stella." Mr. Kensington smiled, pouring himself a cup of coffee.

"Morning, Mr. Kensington." I set my purse down. "Austin, come here." I knelt and held out my arms.

He ran to me like he always did, giving me a big hug. I broke our embrace and gripped his shoulders.

"Go upstairs, get ready for school, and I'll make you eggs in a basket." I smiled.

"Promise?" he asked.

"I promise. Go on." I turned him toward the stairs.

"I've yelled at him a thousand times to get ready, but he

won't listen," Mrs. Kensington said, throwing her protein powder into the blender.

"When you yell at him, he perceives it as threatening and makes him feel unsafe. When he feels unsafe, he isn't going to listen."

"She's right, Nadine," Mr. Kensington said, leaning against the marble counter, sipping his coffee.

"Oh, be quiet, Brandon. How would you know? It's not like you spend any time with the children."

"I'll go get Jenna out of bed." I left the kitchen and walked upstairs.

Approaching her room, I opened the door, sat on the edge of her bed, and tickled her.

She giggled, trying to push my hands away.

"It's time to get up, sleepyhead." I kissed her forehead, and she felt very warm. "Hey, are you feeling okay?"

She slowly shook her head. "My head hurts, and I have a sore throat."

"I'll be right back." I stood up from the bed, went into the bathroom, and grabbed the thermometer from the medicine cabinet. "Open up." I smiled, sticking the thermometer under her tongue.

I pulled it from her mouth when the beeping sound went off. Looking at it, she had a fever of 102.

"You stay right where you are and get some rest. No school for you today."

"Stella, I'm ready." Austin stood in the doorway. "I want my eggs in a basket."

I stood from the bed and followed Austin downstairs.

"Mrs. Kensington, Jenna has a fever of 102. That's why she wouldn't get out of bed. She told me she has a headache and a sore throat."

"Great." She threw her hands up. "Call the pediatrician and take her in. I have to go. I have a meeting."

"I'll take Austin to school," Mr. Kensington spoke.

Mrs. Kensington kissed Austin's head and stepped onto the elevator. Mr. Kensington looked at me and shook his head.

"I guess I don't get a kiss this morning." A smirk crossed his lips.

My lips formed a small smile as I reached into the cabinet and took the children's Tylenol down. I poured the appropriate dose into the medicine cup and handed it to Mr. Kensington.

"Can you please go give this to Jenna? I need to make Austin's breakfast so you can get him to school."

"Of course." He smiled, taking the cup from my hand, his fingers brushing against mine.

"I want eggs in a basket. I want eggs in a basket," Austin loudly voiced as he slammed the fork on the island.

"We do not slam our forks on the counter," I spoke softly as I took it away from him. Grabbing the iPad, I brought up a math app and set it on the island in front of him. "Practice your math while I'm making your breakfast."

"I hate math!" he shouted.

"Math isn't my favorite either, but you have to learn it. Go on. Show me how smart you are." I smiled.

"Jenna took her medicine like a champion." Mr. Kensington walked into the kitchen. "You do know how much we value you, right?" He walked over to where I stood, making Austin's eggs.

"I know." I smiled.

He placed his hand on my back, and I swallowed hard. He'd been doing that a lot lately, making me uncomfortable.

I had been working as a nanny for the Kensington's for two years and had grown to love the children very much. Austin was eight, and Jenna was six. Becoming a nanny wasn't what I had planned when I moved to New York City, but it was all I could find at the time. I loved children and had been babysitting since I was twelve. I also worked in several daycare centers over the years while going to college and earning my degree.

"Eat up, son. We have to go." Mr. Kensington glanced at his watch.

"I'm going to call the doctor's office and see if I can bring Jenna in," I said as I walked out of the kitchen.

Luckily, there was an opening at noon.

"Come on, buddy. We have to go." Mr. Kensington patted Austin's head.

"I'm taking Jenna to the doctor at noon." I handed Austin his backpack.

"I'll have my driver pick you up and take you," Mr. Kensington spoke.

"You have a good day at school. I'll see you later." I kissed Austin's forehead.

"Bye, Stella!" He waved as he and Mr. Kensington stepped onto the elevator.

Picking up my phone, I sent a text to Mrs. Kensington.

"Jenna has a doctor's appointment at noon."

"Good. I'm going to need you to stay later than usual tonight. I have a meeting and don't know how long it's going to take. I'm sure my husband will be working late as well."

"That's not a problem."

"I knew it wouldn't be. Since you're home with Jenna all day, I need you to do the children's laundry. Gloria is off the next few days visiting her mother."

"I'll make sure it gets done."

I waited for a simple 'thank you' but never received one.

Nadine Kensington wasn't a warm and fuzzy woman. She was demanding, worked long hours at the law firm, and didn't have a maternal bone in her body. Why she even had children was beyond me. I suspected it was for show and status. The Kensington's were very well respected in the upper-class community, and they needed to maintain the image of the perfect family of four.

When I took the kids to the park after school, I sat on a bench and talked with the other nannies. We'd all become friends, and they would share stories—or, should I say, gossip—about the wealthy families they worked for. When they'd ask me questions about Mr. and Mrs. Kensington, I'd come up with something that made them look good. Gossip wasn't my thing, and I was staying out of it.

CHAPTER 2

TWO WEEKS LATER

Stella

"What is going on here?!" Mrs. Kensington shouted when she saw Mr. Kensington help get the glue out of my hair.

"Calm yourself, Nadine." Mr. Kensington turned to her. "The poor girl has glue in her hair. Apparently, Austin wanted to have a glue fight."

She stood and stared at me, narrowing her eyes. Her glare told me her mind was spinning out of control.

"Step away from her, Brandon. Where are the children?"

"They're upstairs in the playroom."

She walked over, arms folded, with a stern look.

"You're fired." She scowled.

"What?" My brows furrowed.

"Nadine, what the hell?" Mr. Kensington shouted.

"Don't 'what the hell' me, Brandon. I know there's more going on here. I see the way you look at her."

"Don't be ridiculous. What is the matter with you?"

"Mrs. Kensington, I—"

"You don't say another word, Stella. I'll put your final

check in the mail. You're dismissed. I will make sure you never work as a nanny for any family in New York again."

"What about the children?" I asked.

"They are no longer your concern. Leave." She pointed to the elevator.

I looked at Mr. Kensington, hoping he'd stick up for me. But he didn't. He knew better than to go up against his wife. I slowly walked over to where my purse was, hooked it over my shoulder, and approached the elevator. Before stepping onto it, I turned and looked at the Kensington's.

"I'm not sure why the two of you even got married or had children in the first place. Do your children a favor and get divorced. It'll do less harm than what you're doing to them right now."

"How dare you!" Mrs. Kensington shouted.

I stepped onto the elevator and stared at them as the doors closed. I didn't regret what I said because it was the truth. Their constant bickering and name-calling were enough to drive anyone crazy.

~

I walked into my apartment and threw my purse down.

"What are you doing home already?" My best friend and roommate, Jordyn, asked.

"Mrs. Kensington fired me." I fell on the couch next to her and grabbed the pint of ice cream and spoon from her hands.

"What? Why?"

"She thought her husband was interested in me, and we were having an affair."

"Why would she think that?"

"When she came home, Mr. Kensington was helping me get the glue out of my hair."

"Honestly, I know that man wants you. You know it, too. Don't deny it."

"It doesn't matter. I would never." I stuck the spoon into the ice cream container.

"I know you wouldn't." Jordyn got up and grabbed two glasses and the wine bottle. "No worries. You'll find another wealthy family to work for."

"I doubt it. Mrs. Kensington said she'll make sure I never work as a nanny in New York City again. I know how that woman operates, and she'll tell all of her friends that I stole from them. Before you know it, I'll be labeled as the nanny thief of New York City."

Jordyn laughed. "You really think so?"

"I know so," I said, lifting the spoon to my mouth. "What am I going to do? I need to find a job."

"You have your savings, so don't worry about it too much."

"That won't last, especially with my half of the rent, utilities, credit cards, and student loans."

"Don't forget our Vegas trip is next month for Morgan's and Howie's bachelor/bachelorette party."

"I haven't forgotten." I sighed.

There was a knock at the door. Jordyn got up from the couch and answered it. Glancing at the door, I saw my boyfriend, Sawyer, step inside.

"Hey." I smiled, jumping up from the couch. "What are you doing here? I thought you couldn't come over tonight." I hugged him.

"Jordyn, can I speak with Stella alone, please?" he asked.

"Yeah, sure. I'll be in my room."

"What's going on?" I stared into his chocolate brown eyes as worry tore through me.

He took hold of my hands and gripped them tightly. Taking in a sharp breath, his eyes stayed fixated on mine.

"Stella, you're a great woman and—" he paused.

"You're breaking up with me, aren't you?" Tears filled my eyes.

"Yeah." He nodded. "I'm sorry. The timing isn't right, and I have so much going on."

"What do you have going on?" I broke free from his grip, planted my hands on his chest, and pushed him back. "Just tell me the damn truth, Sawyer!" I shouted.

"Fine. I met someone else, Stella."

Those words tore through me like a serrated knife cutting into a loaf of bread.

"You're an awesome girl who deserves better than me."

"Where did you meet her?" I calmly asked.

"She's a new assistant at the office. I'm sorry." He looked down.

"You fucking piece of shit!" Jordyn emerged from her room and ran over to him. "Get the fuck out of our apartment! And you're right. She deserves better than you, you corporate man wannabe." She opened the apartment door.

"Again, I'm sorry, Stella."

"Just get out," I said as a tear fell down my cheek.

Jordyn wrapped her arms around me. "You don't need his dumb ass. You can do so much better."

I cried in her arms as she led me to the couch.

"How am I supposed to face him when we go to Vegas? He's the best man."

"You're going to forget about him and move on. A lot of alcohol will help."

"Wow. I got fired and dumped all in a matter of a couple of hours." I blew my nose in the tissue Jordyn handed me.

"Everything happens for a reason. You'll see. Something amazing will come out of all of this."

CHAPTER 3

ONE MONTH LATER

Miles

I sat at the table in my attorney's office as he held my mother's will in his hand.

"I'm sorry for your loss, Miles."

"I appreciate that, Nolan, but we know what kind of woman she was."

"She has left her estate to your uncle."

"What? What about the company?" I shifted in my chair.

"You're not going to like it."

"Just spit it out, Nolan."

"Your uncle was given the temporary position of Chairman and CEO."

"What the fuck do you mean? That company belongs to me!"

"Relax, Miles. She has certain stipulations in place. If you marry within a year and stay married for at least one year, the company will be yours. If not, your uncle will permanently hold the title of CEO, and you will remain the president."

"Excuse me?" My brow arched. "That company is rightfully mine, regardless of my marital status," I shouted, slamming my fist on the table.

"I'm sorry, Miles."

"That woman was out of her mind. Make no mistake, Nolan. I will be contesting that will."

"You can't. She included a no-contest clause. She put this clause in her will a year ago, well before she was diagnosed with cancer. She wasn't being manipulated, there was no technical error, and she had no diminished mental capacity. Also, she already has the company documents signed and in place. There are two copies. One with your name as CEO and one with your uncle's name. It's up to you and how badly you want to take over the company."

"My uncle is an idiot. He makes bad business decisions and will bankrupt the damn company." I stood from my chair.

"Then I suggest you find a wife and closely watch Ben." His brow arched. "There's one more thing. Your mother also stated that you must live together if you choose to marry." He looked down at the will. "She says, and I quote, 'In the event Miles chooses to marry, his new bride will move into his penthouse, and they shall live as a married couple. If he chooses to marry out of deception in order to gain control of Bradshaw Capital, the company documents shall be processed immediately, appointing my brother, Ben Hartman, CEO of Bradshaw Capital.'"

"This is bullshit." I stormed out of his office.

"Miles, you have—" my secretary, Isla, started to speak.

"I don't want to hear about anything," I growled, stepping into my office and slamming the door.

Walking over to the bar, I picked up the bottle of bourbon and poured it into a glass, throwing the liquid down the back of my throat to calm my nerves. My office door opened. My Uncle Ben walked in, took one look at me, and made himself comfortable on my couch.

"I take it you spoke to Nolan," he said.

"Yeah." I poured myself another drink.

"I'm sorry, Miles. I'll be moving into your mother's office this afternoon."

"You know this is bullshit." I pointed at him.

"It's what my sister wanted. You can't contest the will because of the no-contest clause. She didn't like the way you live your life. That's why she put me in charge of the company. I've been faithfully married to Alicia for over thirty-five years, and I have my shit together."

"Good for you." I held up my glass as I walked over to my desk.

"Listen, Miles. You're business smart, and your mother knew it. But you lack being smart outside of the office. Find yourself a good woman and settle down. Make a family of your own. It's good for the soul. I do believe your mother is trying to teach you to be more responsible with your life."

"She had no right doing what she did!" I shouted. "And I am responsible! I've made this company billions over the past seven years! Deals she couldn't make, I did!"

"As I said, you're business smart, but there's more to life than this company."

"Shut the fuck up, Uncle Ben." I shook my head.

"You work for me now, nephew. Watch yourself." He pointed at me, stood from his chair, and left my office.

I was so angry that I threw my glass against the wall. My door opened, and Isla walked in.

"Is everything okay, Miles?"

"No! Nothing is okay!" I shouted and grabbed my briefcase. "I'm leaving for the day." I stormed out of my office.

I texted my driver, Sean, to come and get me. As I waited at the curb, I glanced at my watch. When he finally pulled up, I opened the door and climbed into the back.

"What the fuck took you so long?"

"Traffic, Miles. What's going on? You're in one of the worst moods I've ever seen you in."

"My mother. That's what's going on. She put my Uncle Ben in charge."

"What? Why would she do that?" he asked as he pulled away from the curb. "By the way. Where are we going?"

"To Collin's Tavern. The company only goes to me if I get married within a year and stay married for a full year."

"You're not serious." Sean viewed me from the rearview mirror.

"I'm dead serious, and my uncle is loving every minute of it. That son-of-a-bitch. The company goes to him if I don't marry within a year. If I marry and divorce before a year ends, the company goes to him. I'm royally screwed either way."

"I'm sorry, Miles. I know how tense things were with you and your mother."

"She's the reason I am the way I am. She and my father both. But mostly, her."

Sean pulled up to the tavern. I climbed out and told him he could go home for the day.

"Are you sure? How will you get home?"

"I'll take a cab. Just enjoy the rest of your day." I shut the door and stepped inside the tavern.

Walking up to the bar, I sat on the stool and pulled my phone from my pocket.

"Hey, Miles. What can I get you?" Kelly, the beautiful bartender, asked.

"Bourbon. Make it a triple."

I sent a text to my best friend, Levi.

"Can you meet me at Collin's Tavern?"

"When?"

"Now."

"I can be there in thirty minutes. I'm finishing up a proposal."

"Okay. See you then."

Levi Hudson worked for his father's chain of department stores across the country and would take over when his father retired. We'd been best friends since we met in prep school at the age of thirteen. We graduated together, went to the same university, and both graduated at the top of our class with our MBAs.

"Hey." He smiled, sitting on the stool next to me. "Kelly, I'll have what he's having."

"Coming right up, Levi." She smiled.

"What's going on? Why aren't you at the office?"

I sipped my drink, set it on the bar, and looked at him.

"I need to find a wife."

"Excuse me?" He chuckled.

I told him the events of my meeting with Nolan.

"Damn, Miles. I can't believe that."

"You and me both." I held up my glass and alerted Kelly to refill it.

"This is what we're going to do," he said, placing his hand on my back. "We're going to take a trip to Vegas this weekend for some R&R. Just the two of us. You need to get out of New York for a few days to clear your head. Vegas is the perfect place to do that."

"Maybe you're right. It's been a while since I've been there. Will Laurel let you go?"

"Yeah. She'll be fine with it. Don't worry about her."

~

Three Days Later

I boarded my company plane, took a seat, and glanced at my watch. Levi was late as usual, and it pissed me off.

"Good morning, Mr. Bradshaw," Karla, the flight attendant, spoke.

"Morning, Karla. Coffee, please."

"Of course." She nodded.

I heard voices, and when I turned my head, I saw Levi and Laurel step onto the plane.

"What the fuck," I mumbled.

"Hi, Miles." Laurel smiled.

I stood from my seat. "Laurel, what a nice surprise!" I kissed her cheek and looked at Levi. He shrugged.

"When Levi told me you asked him to go to Vegas for a little R&R, I wanted to join in on the fun. I hope you don't mind, Miles." A devilish smile crossed her lips.

"No. Of course not, Laurel. You're always welcome."

"I'm going to use the restroom before we take off." She walked away.

"Really?" I cocked my head at Levi as we sat down. "I invited you? You lied to her."

"It's a little white lie. If I would have told her it was my idea, she would have bitched and moaned that it's been forever since I took her somewhere."

"You just took her to Aruba six months ago," I said.

"To her, that's forever." He rolled his eyes.

"That right there," I pointed at him, "is why I don't get involved in relationships. Women are enough to drive a man to the point of no return and one foot in the door of an insane asylum. Not to mention they are ungrateful and selfish."

"Come on, man. That's not true. Laurel and I have a great relationship."

"Then why did she insist on coming? It's because she doesn't trust your ass."

"Shush. Here she comes. Hi, baby." He smiled, and I rolled my eyes.

I should have known Laurel would impose on our guy's weekend. Now, I felt like a fucking third wheel, and I wasn't happy about it. I was looking forward to spending a few days in Vegas with my best friend and best friend only.

CHAPTER 4

Stella

"I can't believe you brought your laptop," Jordyn said as we sat on the plane.

"I have a paper due in a couple of days."

"What are you going to do? Sit in the hotel room and study all weekend? This is our time to let loose and have some fun." She reached over and closed my laptop.

"How much fun can we have on a plane? I'm using this time to finish my paper so I can let loose and have fun." I opened my laptop.

"You never told me what happened yesterday when you had lunch with a few of the other nannies," Jordyn said.

"That's because you stumbled into the apartment at one a.m., and I was already asleep." A smirk crossed my lips.

"My date with Greg went better than I thought it would." She grinned. "So, tell me what they said."

"Exactly what I said the day she fired me. She's telling her rich, snobby friends that I stole from them, was hitting on her husband, and that I wanted to have sex with him." I typed away on my computer.

"That bitch. I'd sue her for slander."

"Like I can afford to hire an attorney. I can barely afford this trip. Tuition is due next month, and it's going to take a chunk of my savings."

"Well, this trip will take your mind off everything."

"Unlikely." I sighed.

We arrived in Vegas. As we were checking in, Jordyn hooked her arm around me.

"Don't look, but Sawyer just walked in with that whore."

"He brought her?" My belly sank.

"I guess so. You're not going to let that bastard ruin your weekend or fun. Understand me?"

"Sure." I rolled my eyes.

"Hey, Stella." Sawyer walked over to where I stood.

"Why are you talking to her?" Jordyn cocked her head. "Step away, cockroach. Stella and I have a reputation to uphold."

He shook his head and walked away. I couldn't help but laugh.

"That's my girl." She winked.

We went up to our room, and Jordyn immediately changed into her bikini.

"What are you doing?" she asked as I sat on the bed with my laptop.

"I'm almost finished with my paper. You go and meet the girls down at the pool. I'll catch up with you in a few minutes."

"You better." She pointed at me before leaving the room.

I finished my paper and submitted it to my professor. After changing into my bikini, I threw on my cover-up, slipped into my sandals, grabbed my bag, and left the hotel room. Walking down the long hallway, I realized I had gone the wrong way to the elevators.

"Shit," I quietly spoke, turning around.

When I turned the corner, my body collided with another. As I stumbled back, his hand gripped my arm, and his phone hit the floor.

"Oh my God. I'm so sorry." I froze, staring into his blue eyes.

"It's my fault. I was looking down at my phone. Are you okay?"

"I'm fine." I reached down and picked up his phone.

"Thanks. You didn't have to do that. I could have picked it up."

"You're welcome. I ran into you. My fault."

"We ran into each other." The corners of his mouth curved into a sexy smile.

"I guess we did." I grinned. "Are you staying here in this hotel?"

"I am. Why?"

"I'm turned around and can't seem to find my way to the pool."

His eyes raked over me from head to toe.

"Take this hallway down to the end, make a right, and take the elevator down to the ground level. You'll see the pool when you step off."

"Great. Thank you." I bashfully smiled.

"You're welcome—"

"Stella."

"You're welcome, Stella. Have fun in the pool."

"Thanks—" I cocked my head.

"Miles."

"Thanks, Miles."

I gripped the strap to my bag and slowly walked away from the six-foot-three strikingly handsome man—perfectly styled short dark hair, piercing blue eyes, and a ruggedly handsome face with a chiseled jawline that was accentuated by a well-maintained five o'clock shadow. Not only did his looks grip me, but also the scent that radiated from him—earthy, clean, masculine.

"Damn." I shook my head as I stepped onto the elevator.

"It's about time," Jordyn said, patting the lounge chair next to her.

I said hi to Morgan and the other girls before sitting down.

"I got lost."

"What do you mean?" Jordyn's brows furrowed under her oversized sunglasses.

"I took a wrong turn."

"You're here now, and that's all that matters. I ordered you a margarita." She reached over to the table next to her and handed me the glass.

"Thanks."

Reaching into my bag, I put on my sunglasses and stared at Sawyer and his new girlfriend as they stood in the water by the edge, drinking and having a conversation.

"I told him not to bring her," Morgan said.

"It's fine." I sipped my drink. "He's a loser anyway."

"That's my girl." Jordyn grinned.

I couldn't stop thinking about Miles, the man I bumped into. A smile crossed my lips, and Jordyn noticed.

"Why are you smiling?"

I didn't want to tell her about him because I was positive I wouldn't see him again.

"I'm just happy my paper is done, and now I can relax," I said, glancing at her.

"That's the spirit! We're going to have so much fun this weekend."

I saw Miles heading toward me as I sipped my margarita

and took in the sun's extreme heat. My belly flipped with nerves as he approached.

"I see you found the pool." His handsome smile captivated me.

"I did." I smiled as his eyes stared at my bikini-clad body.

"Good. Maybe I'll see you around."

"Yeah. Maybe." I bit down on my bottom lip.

He walked away and down toward the other end of the pool, where he sat with another man and woman.

"Who the hell was that?" Jordyn asked as she slowly took down her sunglasses.

"His name is Miles. We bumped into each other when I was lost and trying to find the elevators to get to the pool."

"And you didn't mention him, why?" She cocked her head.

"I don't know." I shrugged.

"What is wrong with you?" She reached over and slapped my arm. "That man is gorgeous, and you couldn't be bothered to tell me, your best friend, about your little encounter?"

"I forgot."

"Bullshit. That's why you were smiling. You were thinking about him."

I rolled my eyes. "He is handsome, isn't he?"

"Handsome is too kind a word. That man is fucking sexy."

I looked down his way as he chatted with the guy sitting next to him. The woman they were with must have been the other guy's girlfriend or wife.

"Come on, ladies. Let's go back to our rooms, change, and play some slots before we head out later to the clubs," Morgan said.

I really didn't want to play slots because I couldn't afford it, but if I didn't, Jordyn would be up my ass.

We headed back to the room. I changed into a sundress, threw some cash, my license, and my phone into my small purse, and headed down to the casino. I wasn't having any luck with the machine I was on, so I told Jordyn I was going to the other side to find a different machine.

"Go ahead. I'm doing pretty good. I'll find you." She smiled.

Sitting down at another machine that caught my attention, I put in a fifty-dollar bill and bet the minimum. Finally, I'd gotten the bonus and knew I was going to win. I could feel it.

"Oh, come on," I said, as it wasn't paying a penny.

When the bonus was completed, I looked at the winnings, which said zero. Twenty fucking spins, and I'd won nothing —zero, zilch, nada.

"You piece of shit!" I banged on the machine.

"I'm sure the casino wouldn't appreciate you breaking their machine," a low, rugged voice said from behind.

Turning around, Miles stood there with a smile. He took the seat next to me.

"Twenty spins, and I didn't win a penny. That is bullshit. Total bullshit."

He chuckled. "That's the reason I only play the tables."

"Well, I can't afford to play the tables. Hell, I couldn't even afford to put in the fifty dollars this machine stole from me."

"Then why are you in Vegas?" he asked.

"Bachelorette party." I sighed.

CHAPTER 5

Miles

She was beautiful—all five feet eight inches of her. When I ran into her in the hallway, I smiled, and when I saw her at the pool, I smiled. I also smiled as I walked by and saw her banging on the machine. Smiling was something I hadn't done in a while.

"A bachelorette party? It's not yours, is it?"

"God, no. I'm just along for the fun. I didn't even want to come, but my best friend, Jordyn, forced me, even though she knows I'm jobless and can't afford it right now."

"I see. Have dinner with me tonight."

"Seriously?" She cocked her head.

"Yes, seriously." A smile crossed my lips.

"As much as I'd love to, I can't. We're going club hopping."

"And how are you affording that? You're jobless." My brow arched.

"I'll just have to keep drinks to a minimum."

"You have to pay to get into the clubs, and the Vegas clubs aren't cheap. Let me save you some money. Tell your friends you're not feeling well and you're staying in. Let me treat you to dinner and all the drinks you want."

"What about your friends?" she asked. "I saw you sitting with them by the pool."

"They won't care. Trust me. Come on. You know you want to have dinner with me." I smirked.

"Okay. I'll have dinner with you. What time?"

"What time are your friends going clubbing?"

"We're supposed to meet down in the lobby at six-thirty."

"Then I'll pick you up in your room at seven-thirty. Will that be enough time for you to get ready?"

"Yes." A beautiful smile crossed her lips.

"Good. We'll dine in one of the restaurants here in the hotel. That way, we won't risk seeing your friends."

"Okay."

"What's your room number?" I asked.

"2410."

"I'll see you at seven-thirty, Stella." I smiled as I stood from my seat and walked away.

I met up with Levi and Laurel, sitting at one of the blackjack tables.

"You two go to dinner without me tonight." I placed my hand on Levi's shoulder.

"What? Why?"

"I'm taking a beautiful woman to dinner."

The corners of his mouth curved upward. "You're wife hunting in Vegas?"

"No, and shut the fuck up. We ran into each other in the hallway when she was trying to find the pool area. She's sexy as sin, and I need to de-stress." I winked. "Wasn't that the reason we came here?"

"Describe her." He smirked.

"Five foot eight, long brown hair, beautiful green eyes, perfect body—anything else you'd like to know?"

"Age?"

"I don't know. I'd say late twenties."

"Good for you. Have fun tonight." He grinned.

"I intend to." I walked away and headed to my suite.

Stella

"I can't believe you're not feeling good," Jordyn shouted as she stood in the bathroom, getting ready to leave.

"It was the drinks and the hot sun." I pulled the covers over my head. "I probably have sun poisoning."

"You do not. We weren't even out there that long." She walked over to the bed and stared down at me. "Are you sure you can't come?"

"I feel really sick. Apologize to Morgan for me."

"Fine. I will. I hope you feel better." She leaned over and kissed my forehead. "Get some sleep. I'll see you later."

The second the door shut, I threw back the covers, took a quick shower, and got ready for dinner with Miles. I felt bad for lying to my best friend, but if I would have told her I was ditching her for some guy I'd just met, she'd be pissed. This trip had been planned for months, and that's all she and the other girls talked about.

After curling the ends of my long brown hair and dabbing on pink lipstick, I slipped into my short, black, fitted dress with thin straps and the black heels I'd brought.

The knock at the door caused an intense fluttering in my belly, for I was nervous as hell. Walking over to the door, I opened it and gulped as Miles stood there in a pair of dark gray designer suit pants and a white buttoned dress shirt with a tie while holding his suit coat over his shoulder.

"Wow." He grinned. "You look beautiful."

"Thank you. Come on in."

"Did your friends buy your story about not feeling well?"

"Yeah, I think so." I grabbed my small purse.

We took the elevator down to Ocean Prime, a well-known, very expensive steakhouse.

"How did you get a reservation for this place on such short notice?" I asked as the hostess seated us.

"The hotel knows me. I can get in anywhere." A smirk crossed his lips.

"Oh." I opened my menu.

The waiter walked over and took our drink order.

"I'll have a dirty martini with vodka, wet and shaken, extra vermouth, and olive brine." I smiled.

"And I'll have a bourbon, neat," Miles said. "A girl who knows how to order a martini exactly the way she wants it."

"Sometimes, they can get it wrong."

"Where are you from, Stella?" he asked.

"New York. Well, I'm really from Florida. I moved to New York a couple of years ago."

~

Miles

She lived in New York. Shit.

"Where about in New York?" I asked.

"I share an apartment with my friend, Jordyn, in Hell's Kitchen. Ever heard of it?"

"Yes, of course." I smiled.

The waiter set our drinks down and took our dinner order. I picked up my glass and tipped it to my lips. I wasn't sure if

I should tell her I also lived in New York. I didn't want to run the risk of her stalking me once we left Vegas, so I quickly changed the subject.

"How's your martini?" I asked.

"It's perfect." A beautiful smile graced her face.

"I assume since you're having dinner with me, there isn't a boyfriend back home? Or maybe there is, and you're being naughty." A smirk crossed my lips.

"Funny you should mention that." She sipped her drink.

"Why is that?" I grabbed a piece of bread from the basket.

"My ex-boyfriend is here in Vegas for the bachelor party. We broke up a month ago."

"You or him?"

"Him."

"I'm sorry to hear that. It's obvious he's a fool."

"That he is." She smiled, setting down her drink. "He met someone else. Whatever. I'm over it."

"As I said, he's a fool. I'm not sure how any man could or would want to break up with someone as beautiful as you."

"Thank you, Miles. You're very sweet." A bashful smile crossed her lips as she looked down in embarrassment.

"I can see a man breaking up with you if you're a little crazy." I winked. "Are you crazy, Stella?"

"Define crazy." She cocked her head.

I chuckled as I held up my glass, signaling our waiter that I needed a refill.

"How about you, Miles? Girlfriend? I don't see a ring on your finger, so I'm assuming you don't have a wife unless you're one of those men who takes it off during trips, pretending to be single."

"I can assure you there's no ring, no wife, and no girlfriend. I'm as single as they come."

"Hmm," she said, narrowing her eyes at me as our waiter set down our food.

"What?" I took a bite of my filet.

"You're an incredibly handsome man. I sense women fall all over you. There's a reason you're single. Maybe you're crazy." She smirked.

"Some days, I think I am." I sighed.

"Dinner was excellent. Thank you for asking me." A smile brightened her beautiful face.

"You're welcome. Thank you for joining me." I reached across the table and took hold of her hand. I had one thing on my mind and one thing only. "I hope you don't mind." I softly stroked her skin.

"Not at all." Her green eyes stared into mine.

"How about we top the night off with a drink back in my suite? There's a bottle of Dom Perignon waiting to be opened."

"Sure. I'd like that."

CHAPTER 6

Stella

I wasn't the type of girl to have sex with a man I'd known less than twelve hours. But I was in Vegas, alcohol was involved, and Miles was too sexy to turn down. Maybe tonight would be the last night I'd see him, or perhaps I'd see him the rest of the time I was here. Regardless, after I left Vegas, I'd never see him again. What happens in Vegas stays in Vegas. They don't call it Sin City for nothing.

We took the elevator up to the top floor.

"Presidential Suite?" My brow arched when we stepped off.

"Of course. I need to be comfortable, and it's definitely comfortable." He winked.

He swiped the keycard and opened the door. Stepping inside, my eyes widened as I took in the suite's size and décor.

"What the actual fuck?" I looked around. "This is my apartment times six."

Miles chuckled, pulling the Dom Perignon from the ice bucket. After pouring two glasses, he handed me one.

"To a beautiful woman and night," he spoke, holding up his glass.

Smiling, I tipped mine to his. He threw it down the back of his throat, set his glass down, and brought his hand up to my cheek.

"I'm going to kiss you now." He leaned in and brushed his lips against mine.

It felt like a thousand lightning bolts soared through my body. Instantly, our kiss turned feral, and before I knew it, my back was against the wall. With one hand locking me in, his other hand traveled up my inner thigh, and his fingers pushed my panties to the side, plunging inside me. I gasped as my heart raced and his lips explored my neck.

"God, you're so wet," he spoke breathlessly as he explored me. "I need to taste you."

He got down on his knees, lifted my dress, and pulled my panties down. His mouth skillfully explored me, causing the waves of pleasure to build up. Not only did I feel it down there, but I felt it everywhere. My entire body trembled with delight. As my fingers tangled in his hair, the eruption of an orgasm was near. The soft moans that came from my lips intensified as my body tightened and the rush of warmth took over me.

"That was incredible." He stood up and smashed his mouth against mine.

I ran my hand along the length of his hard cock that poked through the fabric of his pants. It felt big, and I couldn't wait to see what I was in for. He grabbed my wrist and held it with a smile.

"There will be plenty of time for you to explore my cock," he spoke. "But first, I need to see you completely naked. Take off your dress." He took a step back.

I slid the straps of the dress off my shoulders and shimmied out of it, letting it fall to the floor. He stood and stared at me momentarily, checking out every inch of my body.

"Fuck." He slowly shook his head.

Bringing his hands up to my breasts, he softly kneaded them, tugging at my hardened peaks before bending down and wrapping his lips around them. I threw my head back at the sensation as soft moans escaped me. He picked me up in one swoop and carried me into the bedroom.

"As much as I want to fuck you against the wall, I want to take my time with that beautiful body of yours, and the best way for me to do that is in bed." He set me down on the edge of the bed.

Taking a few steps back, he stripped out of his clothes. Pulling a condom from his wallet, he tossed it on the bed before taking down his underwear. The man had the body of Adonis and was muscular in all the right places. But my eyes stayed on the sight of his perfectly hard cock.

He stepped closer. I was at the perfect height to wrap my lips around him and slowly take him down my throat. His gasp turned into several moans while his fingers twisted in my hair.

"Stop, Stella," he commanded. "I need to be inside you."

~

Miles

The sight of her naked was too much to handle. She had me excited to the point where I thought I was going to explode before being inside her. After putting the condom on, I grabbed both wrists, lifted her arms over her head, and hovered my body over hers while I thrust in and out. Her legs wrapped around my waist while moans escaped both our lips. Her body shook from an orgasm, and as much as I wanted to hold back for a while longer, I couldn't.

Rolling off her and onto my back, I placed my hand over my heart as I tried to regain my breath. Removing the condom, I tossed it over the side of the bed and into the small trash can.

"Wow." Stella grinned, placing her hand on my chest.

The corners of my mouth curved upward as I stared at her and pushed a strand of her hair behind her ear.

"Wow, is right."

"I need to get back to my room before Jordyn does." She sat up.

"I'll go get your dress." I climbed out of bed and slipped on my underwear.

Walking out to the living area, I grabbed her dress and panties and handed them to her.

"Thank you," she smiled.

After she dressed, I walked her to the door.

"How long are you here for?" I asked.

"A couple more days. You?"

"Same." I smiled. "Maybe I'll see you around."

"Yeah, maybe. It was fun, Miles," she said, placing her hand on my chest. "Much more fun than going clubbing." A beautiful smile graced her lips.

I leaned in and kissed her. "It was nice to meet you, Stella."

"You too, Miles." She opened the door and walked out.

Letting out a breath, I walked over to the bar and poured myself a bourbon. She was a good distraction from the chaos that took over my life.

As I lay in bed, I thought about her. Not only did she live in New York, but she was jobless—a story she didn't want to talk about.

The following morning, I headed down to the restaurant to meet Levi and Laurel for breakfast. When Levi saw me, he waved me over to his table.

"Where's Laurel?" I asked.

"Spa day." He sighed. "She's having the works, and it's costing me a fortune."

I chuckled. "You can afford it."

"So, what happened last night with your beautiful woman?" he asked, sipping his coffee.

I picked up the stainless steel carafe from the table and poured some coffee into my cup.

"Her name is Stella, and she lives in New York, Hell's Kitchen, to be exact."

"Did you fuck her?" A smirk crossed his lips.

"I did." I smiled. "I was up all night thinking about things. Bradshaw Capital is my company, not my uncle's."

"There's only one way to rectify that situation, my friend."

"Stella doesn't have a job."

"Why?" His brows furrowed.

"She said it was a long story and didn't want to discuss it."

"Let's go up to the buffet, get our food, and we can talk about it. I'm starving," Levi said.

"I can't do it, Levi. I can't get married. The last thing I want is a wife."

"Then you can kiss your company goodbye, Miles. You'll forever be stuck as the president and not the CEO. Your uncle will sit in your mother's office, running the company as he wants. Are you really going to let that happen? The fake marriage would only be for a year. Time flies as it is, my friend. Before you know it, a year has passed, the company is yours, and then you can file for a divorce. But you need to find the right woman. A woman you can make a deal with and pay a great amount of money to go along with your sham. A woman who won't fall in love with you." He smirked.

"I know." I sighed.

"It sounds to me that this Stella woman is the perfect candidate. She lives in New York and doesn't have a job. Her new job could be Mrs. Miles Bradshaw." A sly grin crossed his face.

"Shut your mouth." I pointed my fork at him.

I looked up at the restaurant's entrance and saw Stella walk in with her friends. She didn't see me, and I couldn't stop staring at her.

"What the hell are you staring at?" Levi turned his head.

"That's her. That's Stella."

"Which one?"

"The brunette in the light pink dress."

"That's her? Damn, Miles. She looks like wife material to me. You'd make a cute couple." He grinned.

"Shut up, Levi." I inhaled a breath.

CHAPTER 7

Stella

"I'm glad you're feeling better today," Jordyn said. "You missed one hell of a night last night. Ugh, my head."

"I'm going up to the buffet. Are you coming?" I asked her.

"You go ahead. I'm just going to sit here for a while and drink some coffee."

I stood up from my seat, and as I walked up to the buffet, I saw Miles sitting at a table with his friend. He smiled, and I smiled back. My body still trembled from last night. He was incredible and the best sex I'd ever had in my life. He was the fantasy I never thought existed.

As I was walking around the buffet, plating my food, Miles walked up and stood next to me.

"I need to talk to you. Can we meet later?" he asked.

"Sure, of course. When and where?"

"Two o'clock. My suite."

"Okay. I'll be there." I smiled.

"I'll see you then." He walked away and out of the restaurant.

I returned to the table and handed Jordyn a banana nut muffin.

"Here, I know they're your favorite."

She set her phone down and stared at me.

"What's wrong?"

"I just got an email from the manager of our apartment building. The rent is going up four hundred dollars starting next month."

"What? Why? That place is expensive enough for the whole six hundred feet. I can barely afford it now." I sighed. "Fuck. I need to find a job."

We spent the morning and part of the afternoon at the pool, swimming and soaking up the sun. I kept an eye out for Miles, thinking he'd be hanging out at the pool, but he never showed. Glancing at the time on my phone, it was one o'clock.

"I'm going to head back to the room and change out of my swimsuit," I said as I grabbed my things.

"Why?"

"I'm done with the pool for now. I'll catch up with you girls later." I smiled.

When I reached my room, I quickly showered, fixed my hair, and headed to Miles' suite. I knew why he wanted me to come to his room, and I was more than ready to have a repeat of last night.

"Hi." He smiled, opening the door.

"Hi." I stepped inside.

"Can I get you a glass of wine?" he asked, walking over to the bar.

"Sure."

"Red or white?" he asked.

"White."

He poured me a glass and handed it to me.

"I need to talk to you about something, but first, I need you to tell me more about yourself," he said, pouring himself a drink.

"What do you want to know exactly?"

"You're what? Twenty-seven, twenty-eight?"

"Twenty-seven." I furrowed my brows.

"Do you have a college education?"

"Yes." My brows continued to furrow. I wasn't sure what was going on here.

"Then why are you jobless?" He walked over to me.

"What is with all the questions, Miles?"

"Because I need to know more about you."

"Why? It's not like we'll see each other again after tomorrow."

"Here's the thing, Stella. I also live in New York."

"You do?" My heart started racing.

"Yes. What is your degree, and why can't you find a job?"

"I was a nanny for a wealthy couple living on the Upper West Side. For the past two years, I took care of their two children while they worked ungodly hours and couldn't be bothered to handle the daily tasks of raising their kids. One day, while helping the boy finish his art project for school, he decided to go crazy with the glue. It got in my hair, and when his father came home, he was helping me get it out. The wife came home, saw her husband helping me, and fired me on the spot. The story she told her circuit of wealthy friends was that I stole from them and wanted to have sex with her husband. She told me she'd make sure I never nannied for anyone in New York again."

"You're a nanny?" His eyes narrowed.

"Sort of. I only took the job because the pay was good, and I needed it to pay my tuition."

"Tuition for what?"

"My master's degree."

"Wait a second. You're working on your master's?"

"Yes. From NYU."

"What is your degree in?" he asked, tipping the glass to his lips.

"I have a BS in child psychology. My dream is to become a licensed child psychologist, so I planned to finish my master's and then pursue my doctorate."

"If you have a bachelor of science degree in child psychology, why the hell are you working as a nanny?"

"It's all I could find when I moved here. The Kensington's were impressed by my degree and hired me on the spot."

"Brandon Kensington?" he asked.

"Yeah."

"I'll be damned. You were his nanny?"

"Yes. Do you know him?"

"I know Brandon. We've done business together. Did you sleep with him?"

"God, no!" I loudly voiced. "I would never."

"I know for a fact that he wanted to sleep with you. He isn't exactly faithful to his wife."

"I know." I looked down. "I was recently offered a position as a social worker, but I turned it down."

"Why?"

"Because the system is flawed, the hours suck, the pay sucks, and I wouldn't have time for school. I have two classes left to get my master's degree. The tuition is due next month, and I'm going to have to put it off until after I find a job.

Plus, my friend that I live with just informed me this morning that the rent is going up an extra four hundred dollars."

CHAPTER 8

Miles

This was perfect. She needed money, and I needed a wife.

"I can solve your money problems for you. You can finish up your master's and then focus on your doctorate."

"How?" She laughed.

"I can pay for your schooling, plus give you money to live on."

She stared at me with furrowed brows. "I don't understand what's going on here, Miles. Why would you do that?"

"Because I need a favor from you."

"What kind of favor?" She brought the wine up to her lips.

I threw back the rest of my bourbon and set my glass down.

"I need you to become my wife."

"What?" she shouted and spit out her wine.

I grabbed a napkin and handed it to her.

"Are you fucking crazy?" she asked.

"Just listen to me, Stella."

"No. This is insane." She grabbed her purse and headed towards the door. "You're insane."

"You're going to turn down one million dollars? You have no job and no money. Think about how old you'll be before you ever get the doctorate you want so badly."

She stopped, turned around, and stared at me.

"You wouldn't have to work, and your only focus would be on school," I said. "You need the money, and I need a wife. I'll explain everything if you set your purse down and sit on the couch. Please."

She let out a long sigh, set her purse down, and walked over to the couch.

"Explain, now," she said.

"My name is Miles Bradshaw, and I'm the president of Bradshaw Capital. My mother recently passed away, and instead of leaving the company to me, she put my uncle in charge. Her will stated that if I married within the year and stayed married for a year, the company would go to me. That company is rightfully mine, and I should be sitting in my mother's office, running it, not my uncle."

"Can't you contest the will?" she asked.

"She put in a no-contest clause."

"Why would she do that to you?"

"Our relationship was very strained, and she didn't like how I lived outside of the office."

"And how is that?"

"Being a bachelor, seeing a variety of women, never wanting to settle down. She changed her will when she found out she had terminal cancer. I should have seen this coming. I need my company, Stella."

"I don't know, Miles." She shook her head. "This whole thing is preposterous."

"You don't think I know that? Listen. Our marriage wouldn't even be a real marriage. We'd only be married by a piece of paper. We'd live separate lives. You do your thing, and I'd do mine. After one year, we'd have the marriage annulled, and it would be as if we had never been married. I'll pay you five hundred thousand dollars after we're married and the rest after we get divorced. Think about what you could do with that money, Stella. This arrangement benefits both of us. The only thing I'd need from you is when I have dinners and events to attend. People will want to meet Mrs. Miles Bradshaw."

"And what the hell do I tell my friends?"

"You tell them we met in Vegas, fell in love, and got married. It happens. There is one stipulation."

"What?"

"You'd have to move into my penthouse."

"Why? You said we'd live separate lives."

"And we will. It's just my uncle will be keeping an eye on me. It needs to look real. Honestly, the last thing I want is someone moving in."

"Thanks." She rolled her eyes.

"No offense, Stella. You'd have your own room and come and go as you please. My home would be your home for a year. After that, you'll move out and get your own place."

"And what if I meet someone in a year?"

"I wouldn't stop you from dating. I only ask that you don't bring him back to the penthouse, and I will extend the same courtesy to you."

"I can't believe this." She stood from the couch and walked over to the window. "I'm a fucking psychologist. I know better than this."

"A psychologist with a dream. One million dollars, Stella. And a beautiful penthouse for a year."

Stella

I stood there with my arms folded, looking out into the city. My stomach was tied in knots, and I didn't know what to do. This man was willing to pay me one million dollars to become his fake wife for a year. A year that would quickly pass. I could go to school full-time and get my doctorate. Then, I'd be a fully licensed child psychologist and would be able to easily find the job I always wanted. Maybe I could even start my own practice.

"Fine." I turned around. "I'll marry you."

"Seriously?" His face lit up.

"Yes. As you said, this benefits both of us. When and where?"

"As soon as we return to New York, we can file for a marriage license and marry at the courthouse."

"Ah, the dream wedding I've always wanted."

He walked over and wrapped his arms around me, pulling me into an embrace.

"You can have your dream wedding after our year is up. It's only for one year. Thank you, Stella."

"Sure, Miles." I broke our embrace. "I have to go and tell Jordyn I'm moving out."

"By the way. What is your last name?" he asked.

"Harper."

"Thank you, Stella Harper." A smile crossed his lips as he pulled his phone from his pocket. "Since you're my fiancée, I'll need your phone number."

I rattled it off and heard a ding coming from my purse.

"I just sent you a text. Now, you have my number."

"Thanks. I'll see you later or back in New York." I walked out of his suite.

When I returned to my room, I saw Jordyn lying on the bed. How the hell was I going to tell her that I was getting married?

CHAPTER 9

Stella

"There you are. Where were you?" she asked.

"Talking with Miles." I lay next to her on the bed.

"Who?"

"The sexy man I ran into in the hall yesterday."

"Oh. Are you sure you were talking or doing something else?" She grinned.

"We need to talk," I spoke with seriousness.

I told her everything. I told her about how I had dinner and sex with him last night. After I dropped that bomb, I dropped the other one.

"Why aren't you saying anything?" I asked.

"I think you're crazy, but you need to do it. Fuck. There's something I need to tell you. I've been holding back because your life is a mess, and I didn't want to add to it."

"What are you talking about?" I stared at her.

"I got a job offer as a marketing manager in Connecticut. The money was too good to turn down, so I accepted."

"And how long have you known this for?"

"I found out the day before we came here. I didn't want to

ruin our trip. I was going to tell you when we got back to New York."

"You were just going to leave me in that apartment when you knew I didn't have a job and could barely afford to pay my half?"

"Well, I was going to ask you to move with me. I'm sure you'd be able to find a job in Connecticut. But now, you're getting married with five hundred thousand dollars deposited into your account, and I don't have to worry about you."

"Wow, Jordyn."

"I'm sorry, Stella. You know I love you, but I have to take this job."

"I know. But you're moving out of state. You're my best friend. What am I going to do without you?"

"I'll only be two hours away. That's nothing. We'll see each other still. Plus, we can Facetime every day. Besides, you'll have your husband to keep you company." A smirk crossed her lips.

"Stop it. He's only my husband on paper."

She shrugged. "You'll be living with him in his fancy penthouse. You're moving on up, girl. You went from being fired, jobless, and broke to marrying a billionaire and becoming rich all in a matter of a month."

"It feels wrong." I looked down.

"All I can say is if some sexy as fuck billionaire offered me a million dollars to become his fake wife, I'd jump on it, not feel guilty, and lay on the bed naked, rolling in all that cash." She grinned.

"Stop it." I laughed, playfully smacking her.

"Come on. We have to get ready to go out. Unless your fiancé wants you all to himself."

"Very funny."

Miles

It was our last night in Vegas. I hadn't seen or spoken to Stella since our conversation yesterday. I needed time to collect my thoughts and get things in order before I became a married man for the next year. Staring at myself in the mirror as I buttoned up my shirt, I cursed my mother for doing this to me.

I met Levi in the restaurant for dinner at seven p.m. When I approached the table, I saw he was alone.

"Where's Laurel?"

"She has a migraine. So, it's just the two of us tonight." He grinned.

"Good. It's not good that she has a migraine. I do hope she feels better. But it's good that it's just the two of us. There's something I need to tell you."

Our waitress walked over and set a glass of bourbon down in front of me.

"I took the liberty of ordering you one." Levi smiled.

"I appreciate it. Thanks, my friend." I picked up the glass and brought it to my lips. "I'm getting married, and I would like you there."

"Excuse me?" He began choking while sipping his Manhattan. "You're really going through with it?"

"I have no choice, do I?"

"Can I safely assume it's the hot brunette you slept with? What's her name again?"

"Stella Harper." I sighed.

"You said she doesn't have a job, right?"

"No, she doesn't. Get this. She used to be the Kensington's nanny. Nadine fired her and then told all of Manhattan that she stole from them and wanted to sleep with Brandon."

"Did she sleep with Brandon? It wouldn't surprise me."

"She said that she would never. And she didn't steal from them either. Nadine was being Nadine," I spoke, rolling my eyes. "Anyway, Stella has a BS in child psychology."

"That's weird. And she took a job as a nanny?"

"She's finishing up her master's and going for her doctorate." I sipped my bourbon.

"Beautiful and smart." Levi grinned. "You did well, my friend. When is the big day?"

"I'll let you know when we return to New York. I have to file for the marriage license and set a date at the courthouse."

"Uncle Ben isn't going to be happy about this." A smirk crossed his lips.

"Uncle Ben can kiss my ass. I only have to stay married for a year. In fact, once I take over as CEO, and the company belongs to me, I'm firing his ass."

After we ate, we went to the casino and sat at the poker tables. It was midnight when I returned to my suite. Pulling my phone from my pocket, I sent Stella a text.

"What are you doing?"

"I just got back to my room and heading to bed."

"You can head to my bed. See you in five."

"See you in five."

I smiled when I read her last text. Just because our marriage was going to be a sham, sex with her wasn't. The night we shared was more than I'd hoped for, and I wanted a repeat.

My cock spasmed when I heard the knock on the door. I opened it and saw her standing there in one of the hotel's robes and slippers. Instantly, my cock stood at full attention, knowing she was completely naked underneath.

"Get in here." I grabbed her arm, pulled her inside, and up against the wall, locking her body in with mine.

A smile crossed her beautiful lips, and her arms wrapped around my neck.

"I'd say you're happy to see me judging by the hardness against my thigh."

"When you come to my suite in nothing but a robe, yes." My hand traveled in between her legs, and my fingers caressed her slick opening. "I'm not waiting." I dipped a finger inside and smashed my mouth against hers.

Her moans heightened my excitement, as did the continuous wetness that emerged from her. While exploring her, I took my other hand and stuck it inside her robe, groping her breast and feeling her hardened peaks between my fingers. Untying the belt of her robe, I slid it off her shoulders and stared at her beautiful body.

"My turn." She smiled, taking my pajama bottoms down and wrapping her slender fingers around my hard, throbbing cock.

I threw back my head and gasped at her touch, taking in the overwhelming pleasure. The condoms were in the bedroom, and I didn't want to stop.

I stared into her eyes. "Are you on birth control?"

"Yes. I'm on the pill."

"Good. I don't want to stop this to get a condom. I'm one hundred percent clean. I promise you."

"I trust you, Miles." A soft smile made its way to her lips.

Raising her arms above her head, I gripped her wrists with my hand, brought her leg up to my waist, and thrust inside. I lost my breath the moment I felt her without a condom on. Staring into her eyes, I thrust in and out at a rapid speed, my gaze never leaving hers until our lips tangled in pleasure, causing us both to explode. My breath was ragged, and my heart beat at the speed of light. I lowered my head and buried my face into the side of her neck as I let go of the grip that held her. Her arms wrapped tightly around me, and we stood there for a few moments.

"You and your friend Jordyn will be flying home with me tomorrow on my company jet," I whispered in her ear.

"Are you serious?"

"Yes." I took a few steps back, reached down, and slipped her robe on her.

"I don't know what to say. Thank you."

"You're welcome." My thumb traced her lips. "I'll have a driver meet you in the lobby at nine a.m. and take you to the hangar."

"Okay."

I inhaled a sharp breath as she lifted her hand and softly stroked my cheek.

"Go and get some sleep." I opened the door.

"Goodnight, Miles."

"Goodnight, Stella."

I lay my forehead against the door, wondering what the hell I was doing.

CHAPTER 10

Stella

I was exhausted when I returned to my room between partying with the girls, the alcohol I consumed, and having wild sex with Miles.

"What are you doing?" Jordyn mumbled.

"I just got in. Go back to sleep."

I pulled back the covers of my queen bed, climbed in, and fell right to sleep.

My eyes flew open the following morning when it hit me that I didn't take my birth control pill last night.

"Shit!" I quickly sat up.

"What's wrong?" Jordyn let out a long stretch.

"I forgot to take my birth control pill last night. It was so late when I came in, and I was exhausted."

"You'll be okay. Just go take it now and the other one tonight." She rolled over.

I climbed out of bed, used the bathroom, and when I went to grab my pills from the bathroom counter where I left them, the packet was gone. Furrowing my brows, I searched the bathroom. Panic started to set in, and I ran over to Jordyn's bed.

"Wake up!" I shook her shoulder. "Have you seen my pills?"

"They were on the bathroom sink yesterday morning when we left for breakfast," she sleepily replied.

"They aren't there, Jordyn!"

"What do you mean?" She pulled the pillow over her head.

"They're gone. I can't find them anywhere, and Miles and I had free sex!"

She threw the pillow to the other side, and her wide eyes stared at me.

"You had sex without a condom?! What is wrong with you?"

"It was the heat of the moment! Oh my God. What am I going to do? Where are they?" I ran around the room, opening every dresser drawer and my bag.

"Calm down," she said.

"Calm down? I can't calm down!" I picked up my phone, opened my period app, and looked at the big fat words scrolling across the screen: FERTILE PERIOD. I held my phone in front of Jordyn's face.

"Oh shit. Okay. Let me call down to the desk and see if they'll send the housekeeper up who cleaned the room yesterday. Maybe she put them somewhere," Jordyn spoke, reaching over and grabbing the room's phone. "Hi, this is Jordyn. Can you tell me who the housekeeper was who cleaned our room yesterday? Yes. I'll hold. Is she here today? Great. Can you please send her up ASAP? We need to ask her something. Oh, she is? Thank you." She hung up the phone. "She's right down the hall cleaning one of the rooms. I'll go get her." She slipped on her robe. I held the door open while

Jordyn went to talk to her. Within a moment, she walked back with her.

"Hi." I smiled. "Yesterday morning, I had a pack of birth control pills on the bathroom counter. Now, they're not there. Do you remember seeing them when you were cleaning the bathroom?"

"No." Her tone was abrupt.

"Are you sure? Because they were there. I put them there, on the counter, by the sink."

"No. I didn't see any pills."

"Bullshit, lady!" I jammed my finger into her. "They were there. Now they're gone!"

"Whoa, Stella." Jordyn stepped in between.

"If there were pills there, I would have left them."

"Really?" I cocked my head. "And you're telling me that you would have just cleaned around them instead of picking them up and setting them somewhere else?"

"I would have picked them up and put them back down immediately. Maybe you shouldn't be so careless."

"That's it!" I lunged at her, and Jordyn stopped me.

"You're both crazy, and you're slobs, too!" The lady shouted as she walked out of the room.

"Jordyn's the slob, not me!" I yelled.

"Okay. Calm down." Jordyn gripped my shoulders. "There's a CVS around the corner. I'll get dressed and go get you Plan B."

"Thanks, Jordyn." I hugged her.

"No problem." She quickly threw on a sundress and left the room.

"I can't believe we get to fly home on a private jet." Jordyn beamed with excitement. "I like this fiancé of yours." She grinned. "You shouldn't have taken Plan B."

"What? Why would you say that?" I asked, glancing at her.

"Because if you got pregnant, you'd be set for life. Daddy Warbucks would take care of you and his kid for life."

I shook my head as I looked out the window.

We arrived at the hangar where the large plane was waiting. After the driver opened the door, I climbed out and stared at it.

"Mr. Bradshaw is already on the plane," the driver spoke, handing us our bags.

"Thank you." I smiled.

Stepping onto the plane, I couldn't believe my eyes. I'd seen private jets in the movies but never one in real life. It was unlike anything I'd ever seen.

"There you are." Miles smiled, kissing my cheek.

"Hi. Miles, I'd like you to meet my best friend, Jordyn."

"Jordyn, it's nice to meet you." Miles extended his hand.

"The pleasure is all mine, Miles." She grinned. "Thank you for letting us fly home on your private plane."

"You're welcome. Come sit down." He gestured.

"You must be Stella." A man stood from his seat. "I'm Levi, Miles' best friend. This is my girlfriend, Laurel."

"It's nice to meet you." Laurel smiled.

After introductions were made, Miles took my hand and led me to the seat next to his.

"Once we take off, we can go sit on the couch. It's more comfortable."

"This plane is amazing." I smiled.

"Thank you. I'm happy you like it. So, here's the plan.

When we get back to New York, you'll start packing your things to move into my penthouse. I'll take care of the marriage license, and we'll get married at the courthouse on Friday. I'll also need your banking information so I can deposit the first half of the money into your account."

"So, you were the Kensington's nanny?" Levi sat down next to us.

"Yes. I really miss the children."

"Well, won't Nadine be in for a surprise when she hears about your nuptials?" He grinned. "Being Mrs. Miles Bradshaw puts you in a class above her. Damn, this is good." He chuckled.

"Enough, Levi," Miles spoke.

CHAPTER 11

WEDDING DAY

iles

After putting on my suit, I grabbed the small velvet box from the dresser, flipped the lid, and stared at the white gold diamond band—the ring I'd place on Stella's finger. Today would be the day my entire life would change. The thought had me rattled all week. Getting married and having her move in with me was enough to drive me over the edge. This was never part of my life's plan, and my mother knew it. This was just another ploy on her part to ruin my life.

"I can't believe you're going through with this, Miles," my driver, Sean, said as he drove me to Stella's apartment.

"I don't have a choice." I stared out the window.

He pulled up to her building, and I took the elevator up to her apartment. Knocking on the door, Jordyn answered.

"Hello, handsome." She smiled. "Come on in. Your bride is almost ready."

My stomach twisted in a knot at her words. Perhaps I should have brought Stella some flowers. Shit. I wasn't any good at this. I had never been.

"Hi." I heard her voice from behind as I stood in the living room with my hands tucked into my pants pockets.

Turning around, I lost my breath as she stood there in a short, white beaded cocktail dress.

"Wow. You look beautiful." I smiled.

"Thanks."

"Is this everything?" I pointed to her luggage and boxes that sat against the wall.

"Yeah. That's everything."

"The movers are coming to collect your things and bring them to my penthouse. Are you ready to do this?"

"Are you?" Her brow arched.

A small smile crossed my lips as I placed my hand on the small of her back, and we left the apartment.

Levi and Jordyn were our witnesses. I slipped the diamond band on Stella's finger, and she slipped the black tungsten band on mine. When the magistrate pronounced us husband and wife, I inhaled an uneasy breath. Leaning in, I softly kissed Stella's lips.

"Congrats, you two." Levi smiled. "Never thought I'd see this day." He patted my back.

"Be quiet. You know it's not real."

"I tend to disagree with you, my friend. I can't wait until you introduce your wife to your uncle tomorrow night."

"I don't want to think about that right now." I sighed.

Sean drove Stella and me back to my penthouse.

"Welcome to your new home for the next year," I said as we stepped off the elevator.

S tella

My new address was on Park Avenue, Penthouse 16B. I stepped off the elevator and lost my breath at the beauty of the home that was mine for the next year. A grand foyer with beautiful Parquet wood floors and floor-to-ceiling windows with the most spectacular view of the city and Central Park.

"How big is this place?" I asked.

"It's thirty-five hundred square feet with three bedrooms and four bathrooms." He smiled.

"Kind of big for a bachelor, don't you think?" I glanced at him as he showed me around the monstrous place.

He chuckled. "It was in foreclosure, and I got a hell of a deal—too good to pass up. This is your room. Feel free to decorate it any way you want."

"It's beautiful the way it is." I smiled.

"Monday, Dora, my maid, will be here. She works Monday through Friday. You'll like her."

"She's not working today?"

"Under the circumstances, I gave her the day off. "Come on. I'll show you the other wing where my bedroom is located." He took hold of my hand.

"Wow. Your room is double the size of my apartment." I smiled.

"And my bed is very comfortable." He reached around and unzipped my dress. "We do need to consummate our marriage." He slid the dress off me.

"Yeah. I think we do." I wrapped my arms around his neck.

Before I knew it, he had me lying on the bed, fully naked, exploring me with his mouth as my body trembled. He thrust inside me as his muscular body hovered over me. Intoxication took over as our lips tangled and his thrusting increased. I was in such bliss that I didn't even realize he forgot to use a condom. Shit.

"God, that was good," he breathlessly spoke, pulling out of me and rolling onto his back.

I looked over at him. "You didn't use a condom."

"Why would I? You're on the pill. We didn't use one last time." He reached over and softly stroked my cheek. Sitting up, he pulled on his underwear. "We need to go over some rules, Stella."

"Okay." I held the sheet against me as I sat up.

"This marriage isn't real, and it can never be. We made an arrangement, and now you're five hundred thousand dollars richer."

"I know that, Miles."

"I don't answer to you, and you don't answer to me. We live our separate lives for the next year."

"I'm fully aware of that."

"Okay. I just want to make sure you understand that. Get dressed, and I'll show you my office."

I furrowed my brows as I slipped on my white beaded cocktail dress and followed him.

"You can use this office anytime you want for your studies," he spoke. "As long as I'm not using it. I do a lot of work in here at night."

"Okay. I have my laptop, so I can do my studies anywhere."

"My driver, Sean, will be available when you need him as long as I don't. If he's not available, take a cab. I don't want you to take the subway. Understand?"

"Yes." I smiled. "I won't take the subway."

"Good." He kissed my forehead. "Tomorrow night, we're meeting my Uncle Ben for dinner, so you'll need a nice dress. I'm unsure if you have any, so I want you to buy one at Bergdorf's. You can put it on my account there."

"Okay."

He gripped my hips. "I have to go into the office. I'll be home later. Get unpacked and make yourself comfortable."

"I have homework to catch up on." I smiled.

"That's good. Your studies are important. I'll see you later."

After he left, I went into the open sun-flooded kitchen with Glasso's countertops, custom white cabinetry, two oversized sub-zero refrigerators, top-of-the-line stove, and four built-in ovens, graced the chef's kitchen. This was every woman's dream. I opened the fridge and saw it was fully stocked with meats, fruits, and vegetables. Grabbing a bottle of water, I took it to my bedroom and changed into more comfortable clothing.

I stared at the diamond band on my finger, which alerted me that I was now Mrs. Miles Bradshaw. I barely knew my husband, and even though this was a marriage of convenience, I really didn't know anything about him.

I walked up the marbled staircase in the hallway, which led to a room with a sectional, TV, a large bar, and a black baby grand piano. A glass door led to the rooftop terrace, which housed potted plants, lounge chairs, and a large outdoor table set. I stood and stared at the view of the city. It was indescribable, and I could see myself doing a lot of studying out here, at least in the warmer months.

CHAPTER 12

Miles

"Your uncle was looking for you," Isla said as I walked into my office.

"I'm sure he was. What did you tell him?"

"That you were across town for an appointment." She glanced at my finger.

Isla was not only my secretary; she was my right-hand person. She kept me organized. She was valuable to me, considering she worked for me for the last six years. She knew some of my secrets, and I trusted her with my life. Besides, she was in with my plan because she would move up when I took over as CEO.

"So, how did it go?" she asked.

"As good as any courthouse marriage."

"I can't wait to meet her."

"You will in time. I need those reports. I know that's why my uncle wants to see me."

"They're right there on your desk." She pointed.

"Thanks, Isla." I smiled, took off my ring, grabbed the reports, and headed down to see my uncle.

Stepping inside, he looked up from his computer. The sight of him sitting in that chair made me sick.

"I was looking for you," my Uncle Ben said as he leaned back in his chair.

"I know. I was out of the office."

"Where were you?" he asked.

"I had an appointment. Here are the reports you wanted." I set them on his desk.

"Thanks. I had a meeting this morning with Walsh Industries." He picked up the bottled water from his desk.

"What?" I narrowed my eyes. "We were supposed to meet with them first thing Monday morning."

"Yeah, well, Yuri called and said he couldn't make it on Monday, so we met this morning. If you would have been here, you would have known."

Fuck.

"And?" I cocked my head.

"It's a traditional Series A deal, Miles. The company is pulling in three million a year. I looked over the comps, and I think this particular company can be valued at ten times ARR."

"That could be so, but their customer concentration is too high. I pulled the reports, and they've lost a lot of customers over the last two years," I said. "If we were to take twenty-five percent control of the company, maybe."

"He won't agree to that," he said.

"Schedule another meeting for next week so I can talk to him."

"No need. I already told him we'd invest with one percent controlling interest."

"Are you out of your mind?" I shouted.

"Don't forget who's in charge here." He stood up from his

chair and grabbed his suit coat. "I have to go pick up your aunt. We'll see you tomorrow night at dinner."

I sighed as I walked out.

My phone rang as I was sitting in my office. Glancing at it, my brows furrowed when I saw it was Stella.

"Hello." I put it on speaker.

"Hi. It's me."

"I know who it is, Stella. What's up?"

"I was wondering what time you're going to be home."

"Why?" I asked.

"I'm cooking dinner."

She was playing the wife role, and it didn't sit well with me.

"Honestly, I have no idea what time I'll be home. I have a lot of work to do."

"Oh, okay. I'll see you when I see you. Bye, Miles." She hung up.

"I heard that," Isla said, standing in the doorway. "Maybe she wanted to do something nice, and you just dismissed it."

I cocked my head at her.

"She doesn't need to cook me dinner. I can get my own. Shut my door."

She rolled her eyes and pulled the door shut.

Sighing, I picked up my phone and texted Stella.

"I can be home by seven o'clock."

"Okay. Dinner will be ready at seven."

~

I climbed into the back of the Escalade, and Sean drove me home. It was seven-thirty when I stepped off the elevator and into the penthouse. Setting my briefcase down, I walked into the kitchen.

"You're late." Stella smiled, holding a glass of wine.

"It was a busy day. I'll go change, and we can sit down to dinner. Unless you already ate."

"No. It's in the warming oven." She smiled.

After changing out of my suit and into more comfortable clothes, I poured myself a bourbon and took it over to the table.

"I made chicken marsala, risotto, and grilled asparagus." Stella smiled, setting my plate before me.

"This looks wonderful. Thank you. You didn't have to cook me dinner." I picked up my fork.

"I know, but I wanted to. Besides, I thought we could get to know each other better. I am your wife and barely know anything about you, Miles."

I stared at her from across the table. She looked beautiful like she always did.

"What do you want to know?" I asked.

"Anything you're willing to share."

"Well, I'm a workaholic. Bradshaw Capital is the reason I get up in the morning."

"I already knew that." A smirk crossed her lips. "I saw the piano upstairs. I assume you play?"

"I do. This is delicious, Stella."

"Thanks. Who taught you?"

"Actually, my father did. He played. Every night, when he got home from work, he poured himself a drink and played the piano for a while. He said it relieved the stress of the day. I would sit next to him when I was a kid, and he'd play a few songs. It was really the only time I got to spend with him. Running Bradshaw Capital was his priority. I used to play soccer, and he never once attended my games."

"Why?" Stella's brows furrowed.

"When I asked if he would be there, he told me he didn't have the time because he was building my future."

"And your mother?"

"She came to a few over the years, but not many. She'd be on her phone the entire time. She and my father were Bradshaw Capital's power couple. That company was everything to them."

"I don't understand why she put your uncle in charge. That company is rightfully yours," Stella said, picking up her wine glass.

"My mother was a narcissist. She never apologized for anything, and she was never wrong. Everything was about her. One day, when I was fourteen, we got into a huge fight. I asked her why she even had me, and she said she had no choice. My father wanted a child who would carry on the family legacy they were building. After I was born, she had her tubes tied so she couldn't have more children. She told my father she gave him a son, and that was enough. From the time I could walk and talk, I attended the best prep schools in New York. It was all about the show and what made her and my father look good. As I said, they were Bradshaw Capital's power couple, and I was expected to uphold their image. Out of defiance, I got into a lot of trouble as a kid and was almost expelled from school. But once my parents made a huge donation, the things I did went away. While I was at Harvard, my father passed away, and my mother took his seat in the company, making my uncle her right-hand man. After I graduated, I went to work for the company. I worked hard, and I would party when I left the office. Levi and I would go to clubs, drink, and pick up different women. I was featured on Page Six daily, and my mother said I was making a fool of myself and tarnishing the Bradshaw name."

"I'm sorry, Miles."

"I eventually cleaned up my act. She wanted me to settle down and give her a grandchild. That was the one thing she couldn't control, and she didn't like it. Hence, the reason she temporarily put my uncle in her position and stated that if I married and stayed married for at least a year, the company would go to me. Even from the grave, she's still trying to control me."

"It worked, didn't it?" Stella said, sipping her wine.

"She knew how important that company is to me. Enough about me. Tell me about your parents?"

CHAPTER 13

*S*tella

"I was born and raised in Tampa, Florida. When I was ten, my parents and I were in a serious car accident that took their lives. After I got out of the hospital, I went and lived with my grandmother. After I graduated from high school, I attended the University of Florida. I got my bachelor's when I was twenty-three, and right before I started the master's program, my grandmother became very ill, and I had to take some time off to take care of her. Six months later, she passed away. After the funeral, Jordyn convinced me to come to New York, move in with her, and get my master's and doctorate at NYU. So, I did. When I was having trouble finding a job that would cover my living expenses and tuition, a friend of a friend of Jordyn's told me that the Kensington's were looking for a new nanny, and I should apply. She said they would pay me well, and I'd still be able to take my classes. I applied, and they were impressed with my credentials. They hired me on the spot."

"I know Nadine, and I can't imagine it was easy working for her." A smirk crossed his lips.

"It wasn't. But the kids made it better." I smiled.

"You really like kids, don't you?" he asked, finishing the last of his bourbon.

"I love kids. I started babysitting when I was twelve and worked in daycare centers while I was in school. Who doesn't love kids?" I got up from the table and grabbed our plates.

"Me, for one," he said, and I stopped momentarily before setting the dishes in the sink.

"You don't like children?"

"Ten and up are okay. Any child under ten, no."

"Why is that?"

"They're loud, obnoxious, demand too much attention, and most of your time. Being responsible for another human being is not my thing."

"So, you never want children?" I turned and looked at him.

"No. My work causes enough stress in my life. The last thing I'd need is to walk through the door after a long workday to a screaming kid. I like my peace and quiet. But I take it you plan on having children someday."

"Yeah, I do because I love kids."

"To each their own." He winked. "We couldn't be more complete opposites." He took hold of my hand. "Except in the bedroom. Leave these dishes for tomorrow morning and come with me." He led me to his bed.

I awoke in my bed the following morning. Miles suggested that it wasn't a good idea that I stayed in his after we had sex. He was a complicated man with a lot of issues. Issues that stemmed from his parents and childhood.

Climbing out of bed, I went into the kitchen, where Miles sat at the island, scrolling on his phone and drinking a cup of coffee.

"Morning," I said, making my way to the coffee machine.

"Morning. How did you sleep?"

"Like a baby. You?"

"Well, babies don't sleep, so I never understand why people use that phrase. I slept great."

I rolled my eyes as I pulled down a mug from the cabinet.

"I'm happy to hear that."

"I'll see you later. I'm going to the office." He set his coffee cup in the sink.

"On a Saturday?"

"It's just another day, Stella." He smirked. "Don't forget we have dinner with my aunt and uncle tonight."

"I know. I'm going shopping today for a new dress."

"Good. I have no doubt you'll look beautiful in it." He grabbed his briefcase and walked to the elevator.

~

"Miles doesn't ever want kids," I said to Jordyn as we walked down Fifth Avenue with our coffee in our hands.

"Okay, and?" She glanced at me.

"Nothing. I'm just saying he doesn't like kids."

"Why do you seem bothered by it? Are you planning on having his baby?"

"Shut up." I laughed. "Of course not. I just think it's sad."

"Are you really surprised, Stella? I mean, he is a man who paid you to marry him so he could get control of his company. A man of his looks and status shouldn't be single. He chooses to be, so I'm not surprised he doesn't want kids. Could you imagine if you got pregnant in Vegas after that whole birth control debacle?" Her eyes widened.

"I don't ever want to think about that again. I really hate that you're moving." I laid my head on her shoulder.

"I know, but things won't change. We'll still talk every day. Have you asked Miles to attend Morgan's wedding with you?"

"Not yet. I'm going to today. I hope he says yes."

She stopped in the middle of the sidewalk and grabbed my arm.

"Are you falling in love with him?"

"No." My brows furrowed. "Why would you think that?"

"Because of the tone you used when you said you hope he says yes. It was like a teenage girl all excited that the guy she'd been chasing down all year asked her to the prom."

"You're crazy." I rolled my eyes. "I think it would be fun. We could dance." I smiled.

"Somehow, I don't think uptight Miles Bradshaw dances."

After a day of shopping, Sean drove me back to the penthouse.

"Thanks, Sean. I'll see you later."

"See you, Stella." He smiled.

When I stepped off the elevator, I heard piano music. Taking my bags to my room, I walked up the winding stairs and saw Miles sitting at the piano.

"Hi." I smiled.

"Hey." He stopped.

"You don't have to stop. It sounds beautiful." I walked over and sat on the bench next to him. "How long have you been home?"

"Not long." He placed his hands on the keys and began playing a soft melody. "Did you find a dress?"

"Yeah, I did. I wanted to ask you something."

"Okay. What is it?"

"My friend Morgan's wedding is next weekend, and I was wondering if you'd like to be my date."

"I appreciate the offer, but no. Weddings aren't my thing."

"Oh, come on, Miles. It'll be fun."

"I said no, Stella." His tone was abrupt.

"Okay." I stood up. "I have to get ready for dinner." I walked down the stairs and to my room.

I couldn't help but feel disappointed. I knew he made it clear that I would live my life and he would live his, but what the hell was the big deal about attending a wedding with me? I had to go to this stupid dinner with him and pretend to be his wife. This arrangement was going to be a lot harder than I thought it would be.

CHAPTER 14

Miles

It didn't matter if I pulled this off or not. All I had to do was stay married for one year, and there wasn't a damn thing my uncle could do.

When Stella emerged from her room, and I turned around, my heart beat faster as I stared at her beauty.

"You look beautiful." I smiled.

"Thank you. I'm ready to go if you are."

I placed my phone in my pocket, and we headed to where Sean awaited us with the car.

"I'm a little nervous." She glanced at me.

"Don't be," I said, taking hold of her hand. "We got this." The corners of my mouth lifted as I gave her a wink.

When we walked through the doors of Tavern on the Green, the hostess took us to the table where my aunt and uncle were waiting for us.

"Hello, Miles." My Aunt Gabby stood and hugged me.

"Hello, Aunt Gabby."

"Miles." My Uncle Ben nodded, extending his hand. "I didn't know you were bringing anyone with you."

"Aunt Gabby. Uncle Ben. I'd like you to meet my wife, Stella."

Immediately, his eyes diverted to our ring fingers.

"Excuse me?" He cocked his head. "Your wife?"

"Oh, dear, Miles. When did this happen?" My aunt asked with surprise.

"Yesterday. Stella, this is my Uncle Ben and Aunt Gabby."

"It's nice to meet you both." She smiled as we sat down across from them.

"What are you up to, Miles?" My uncle's eyes narrowed.

"I'm up to nothing, Uncle Ben. I met Stella in Vegas, and it was love at first sight. We spent the weekend together, and I fell in love and wanted to make her my wife." I smiled.

"Bullshit," he said.

"Ben, please." My aunt placed her hand on his arm.

"It's very nice to meet you, Stella. Welcome to the family." My aunt smiled, reaching across the table and placing her hand on Stella's."

"You were in the office yesterday, and I didn't see a ring on your finger." My uncle glared at me.

"I didn't wear it because I wanted it to be a surprise." I grinned.

The waiter walked over and took our drink order. I needed that drink, and I needed it now.

"Stella is fully moved into my penthouse, and we're very happy. Isn't that right, baby?" I took hold of her hand.

"Yes. The moment I met Miles, I knew he was the one." She leaned over and kissed my lips.

My uncle stared at me, shaking his head. "I knew you'd do something like this, but I didn't think it would happen so quickly. How much is he paying you, young lady? And who the hell just meets someone and marries them a few days later? I'll tell you who. A gold digger." He pointed at Stella.

"You will not disrespect my wife, Uncle Ben. She is a part of this family now."

"You won't make it a year," he said, picking up his drink.

"I appreciate your confidence, Uncle Ben. Now, let's have a nice dinner." I smiled, opening the menu.

~

*S*tella

I was uncomfortable, to say the least. Suddenly, I heard someone yell my name. Glancing over, I saw Austin and Jenna running toward me. I stood from my chair.

"Hey, you two." I smiled, hugging them.

"Stella?" Mr. and Mrs. Kensington approached me. "What are you doing here?" he asked.

"We miss you so much, Stella." Jenna pouted.

"Miles." Mr. Kensington extended his hand.

"It's good to see you, Brandon. Nadine, you look as lovely as ever."

"Is she with you?" Mrs. Kensington asked.

"I am, Nadine." I stared at her.

"Stella is my wife. We were recently married," Miles spoke.

"Excuse me?" Mr. Kensington asked. "I don't—"

"I didn't realize you two were dating," Mrs. Kensington said.

"We met in Vegas, and it was love at first sight." A smile crossed my lips.

"Please come back to us," Austin whined. "We hate our new nanny."

"Austin, that's enough," Mrs. Kensington scolded him.

"Congratulations to the both of you," Mr. Kensington said. "Come on, children. We must go back to our table."

"No!" Jenna shouted, hugging me tightly. "I want to stay with Stella."

"Me too!" Austin shouted, causing a scene in the restaurant.

"Listen to me." I knelt in front of them. "I miss both of you so much, but I have to focus on my schooling now. Remember how I told you I was taking classes to become a doctor?"

They both nodded as their sad eyes stared into mine.

"I need to go to school full-time so I can make that happen. Just like the two of you go to school."

"It's not fair. We don't like our new nanny," Jenna whined.

"That is enough, Jenna!" Mrs. Kensington spoke sternly. "Let's go."

I gave the children another hug and watched them head to their table. Sitting in my chair, I sighed and picked up my Cosmopolitan.

"You were the Kensington's nanny?" Uncle Ben asked.

"Yes. For two years."

"What type of doctor are you studying to be?" Aunt Gabby asked.

"I'm going for my doctorate in child psychology. I'm finishing up my master's now."

Uncle Ben chuckled. "You're a psychologist and married him?" He pointed at Miles.

"As I said, it was love at first sight."

"Yeah, right." He shook his head. "You know what? I think it's time we head home, Gabby." He stood from his chair.

"We haven't had dinner yet," Miles said.

"Suddenly, I've lost my appetite. Let's go, Gabby."

"He hates me." I stared at Miles, who sat there with a grin on his face.

"He doesn't hate you. He hates me because he knows his time is limited at Bradshaw Capital. I guess it's just the two of us." He held up his drink.

Our waiter approached the table and set our food down.

"The two that were with us left," Miles said.

"Oh. Okay. I'll just take their food back to the kitchen."

Miles

"Excuse me for a moment, Stella," I said, getting up from my seat.

I walked over to the Kensington's table. "Why don't the two of you go over and talk to Stella before we leave?" I said to the children.

They quickly exited their seats and ran over to our table. I sat down across from Nadine and Brandon.

"Stella is a good woman. You made the right choice, Miles," Brandon said.

"Shut up, Brandon." Nadine sipped her drink.

"Stella told me what happened and why you fired her, Nadine. She also told me the rumors you're spreading about her throughout the social circle."

"That woman is a thief, and she was after my husband."

"You're a liar." I pointed at her.

"How dare you, Miles?"

"She didn't steal from you and wasn't after Brandon. I don't appreciate lies and false information being spread about my wife. You tell your social circle that you were wrong in firing Stella. Understand me?"

"I will do no such thing," Nadine scolded.

"Okay then. Maybe your social circle would like to know the kind of financial trouble you're in."

"Now hold on, Miles." Brandon raised his hand.

"You wouldn't dare." Nadine's eyes narrowed.

"Oh, but I would." I smiled. "She's my wife, and I will not tolerate lies being spread for something she didn't do because of your insecurities, Nadine. She still talks to the other nannies. So, next time she does, she better tell me that you told everyone you were wrong, and you regret firing her." I stood from my chair. "Enjoy the rest of your dinner." I walked back to my table. "Austin. Jenna. Your parents are waiting for you."

"Bye, Stella." Both children waved to her.

"What did you say to them?" Stella asked.

"Nothing you need to worry about." I picked up my fork.

CHAPTER 15

ONE MONTH LATER

*S*tella

My eyes flew open at the sudden feeling of nausea that took over me. Jumping out of bed, I ran into the bathroom and leaned over the toilet. Shit. Not today. I started my new semester at NYU. As I sat on the floor with my head in the toilet, I could feel the rise in my throat. When it was finally over, I stood up, grabbed a wash cloth, ran it under hot water, and placed it on my face. The nausea was still there, but not as bad.

I stepped into the shower and quickly shaved and washed my body.

"Good morning." Mile's voice startled me.

"Miles, what the hell?"

I turned off the shower, and he was standing there holding a towel when I slid open the door.

"Thanks." I grabbed it and wrapped it around my body. "Why are you in my bathroom?"

"Well, it is my bathroom too. This is my penthouse." He smirked. "Anyway, I know you start your new classes today and I was worried you weren't up yet."

"I am, and I need to get ready." The smell of the coffee he held intensified the nauseous feeling in my belly.

"I'll make you a cup of coffee before I leave," he said.

"No, don't."

"Why not?" His brows furrowed.

"I don't feel like any right now."

"You always have coffee first thing in the morning."

"Not today." I walked into the bedroom.

"Okay. I'll see you later. Good luck today." He smiled, kissing my forehead.

"Thanks."

The last two classes I needed weren't available online, so I had to attend class in person, which I was happy to do. I wanted to be around other people and not cooped up in this penthouse all day, which I had been for the last month with my other classes.

The situation between Miles and I hadn't changed. He did his thing. I did mine. When he wanted sex, we did, which was amazing every time. I fell for him back in Vegas and even more now. I was in love with Miles Bradshaw and didn't know what to do.

We weren't your traditional married couple. After sex, I would leave and go back to my room. That's the way he wanted it, and I hated it. I craved his body wrapped around mine at night, holding me tight and making me feel like I was the only woman in the world. He didn't take me out on dates, and I barely spoke to him all day, only when he came home for a few moments before he went into his office and shut the door. What did I expect? I knew this marriage was fake, and I knew Miles would never be able to commit to anything. He was an emotionally damaged man, but I still fell in love with him anyway, being fully aware of the pain and complications that go with loving someone like that.

While I was getting ready, my phone rang with a Facetime call from Jordyn.

"Good morning, sunshine. How is the rich life treating you?" She brightly smiled.

"Morning."

"What's wrong." Her brows furrowed.

"I start classes at NYU today, and I'm not feeling well."

"How?" she asked.

"I threw up when I got out of bed, and I feel very nauseous still."

"The flu is going around. Make sure you stay hydrated."

"Jordyn, I love you, but I have to go." I ran to the toilet and vomited.

"Damn, Stella. How are you going to go to classes?"

"I don't know," I said, my head in the toilet.

"Eat some crackers. I'm hanging up. I'll check on you later to see how you are."

"Okay." I threw up again.

Shit. This was not okay. I wiped my mouth, gripped the counter, and stared at myself in the mirror. Inhaling a deep breath, I felt better. Maybe it was the Chinese food I ate last night. I prayed that was it for the rest of the day.

∼

Miles

We'd been married for a month already, and only eleven months remained before I took over as CEO of Bradshaw Capital. My Uncle Ben popped over one night for a surprise visit. I knew it was to see if I was lying about Stella moving in, and I took great satisfaction when he saw her and her things around the penthouse.

My office door opened, and I saw Levi standing there when I looked up.

"Do you have some time for a friend?" he asked.

"Get in here." I smiled as I got up from my chair, walked over, and hugged him. "How was your trip?"

"It was good." He sat down across from my desk. "How's married life?"

I cocked my head at him. "You mean my fake married life?"

"Okay." He chuckled. "Your fake married life."

"It's fine." I leaned back in my chair. "I do my thing, and she does hers."

"Are you sleeping around with other women?"

"Nah. There's no need to when I can have it anytime I want at home." A smirk crossed my lips.

He sat there, narrowing his eyes.

"What's that look for?"

"Nothing. Anyway, I have some news. I proposed to Laurel, and she said yes." He smiled.

"Wow, Levi. Congratulations. I'm happy for you. If that's what you really want."

"Of course it is, Miles. I love her and want her to be my wife—my real wife with a real relationship for the rest of our lives."

The way he said that struck a nerve in me.

"When's the big date?" I asked.

"We haven't set one yet. But when we do, I want you as my best man."

"I would be honored." I smiled.

"And you better bring your wife." He pointed at me. "Fake marriage or not."

"Can you please stop calling her that. It's not real, and you know it. I still consider myself single."

"I hate to break the news to you, my friend, but it is real. You have the rings and the marriage license to prove it. I will keep calling her your wife as long as you have those." He stood up. "I have to get to the office. I just wanted to stop by and tell you the big news."

I walked over and hugged him. "Congratulations, Levi."

"Thanks, Miles."

He walked out of my office and shut the door. I walked over to the window, tucked my hands into my pants pockets, and stared out at the busy city. I thought about Stella. Picking up my phone, I sent her a text.

"How are classes going?"

I waited for a response, and after a few moments, I placed my phone in my pocket and headed to a meeting. Once my meeting was over, I pulled out my phone, and still no text from her. What the fuck? I called Sean.

"Hey, Miles."

"Did you pick up Stella at NYU yet?"

"Yes, and I drove her straight home."

"How long ago?"

"About an hour."

"Was she okay?"

"Yeah. She was fine. Why?"

"Just wondering. I'm leaving the office around five o'clock."

"Okay. I'll be there."

CHAPTER 16

Stella

I'd made it through the day, but damn was I tired. Stepping off the elevator, I kicked off my shoes, set my bag down, and walked into the kitchen.

"How was your day?" Dora smiled, wiping down the island.

"It was good. I'm going to enjoy these last two classes."

"You look tired, Stella. Can I make you some tea?"

"That would be great, Dora. Do we have any peppermint tea?"

"Yes." She smiled.

She made me some tea and set it down before me at the island. Holding the warm cup between my hands, I took a soothing sip.

"Are you okay?" she asked.

"Just feeling a little under the weather today."

"I made dinner for you and Miles. It's in the warming oven." She grabbed her purse.

"Thanks. I'll make sure his stays in there because God knows what time he'll be home."

"I just want you to know that I don't agree with this little arrangement the two of you have. I don't want to see you get hurt."

"It's too late for that." I sipped my tea.

She walked over and placed her hand on my shoulder. "Get some rest. I'll see you in the morning."

I gave her a smile, got up from the stool, grabbed my bag and laptop, and sat down on the couch. When I heard the elevator ding, I looked at the time; it was five-thirty.

"You never responded to my text message," Miles said, strolling into the living room.

"Why are you home so early?" I asked.

"Is there a rule that says I can't come home at five-thirty?"

"No. It's just you're never home this early."

"As I said, you never responded to my text."

"Sorry. I forgot."

"You forgot?" His brow arched.

"I was in the middle of class when you texted me, and I forgot."

"Well, don't forget next time. I had to call Sean to make sure you were okay."

"I'm sorry. It's been a long day. Dora made dinner. It's in the warming oven."

"Did you eat yet?" he asked.

"No. I've been doing homework." I looked up at him.

"I'm going to my bedroom to change. We can eat, and you can tell me about your new classes."

"Okay. I'll go pull it from the oven." I set my laptop to the side and got up from the couch.

I silently smiled as I strolled into the kitchen. We were having dinner together for the first time in over two weeks. I pulled our dinner from the warming oven, plated it, and set it on the table. Grabbing a bottle of water from the refrigerator, I sat down.

"No wine tonight?" Miles asked, walking into the kitchen.

"Not tonight. My stomach has been bothering me all day."

"Are you sick?" he asked, sitting across from me.

"I don't know." I picked up my fork. "I know there's a virus going around, so maybe."

"I'm sure you'll feel better tomorrow. So, tell me about your day." A small smile crossed his lips.

"It was good to attend classes in person. It's been a while." I smiled. "I like my professors."

"I'm happy to hear that. Levi dropped by the office today with some news."

"Oh yeah?" I took a bite of chicken and wanted to vomit.

"He proposed to Laurel and asked me to be his best man. They haven't set a date yet, though."

"That's great. But you don't do weddings. How are you going to be his best man?" A smirk crossed my lips.

"He's my best friend. I have no choice."

"I'm your wife, and you wouldn't attend my friend's wedding with me." My brow arched.

His eyes stared into mine momentarily. "I'm sorry about that. I probably should have gone with you."

"Easy to say now that it's over with." I threw my napkin on the table and stood up.

"Where are you going? You barely ate."

"To my room to do homework." I walked out of the kitchen.

Miles

What the hell was her problem? Something was obviously bothering her, and I wanted to know what it was. After cleaning up dinner, I went into her room and heard the water running from the bathroom. Opening the door, I stepped in and saw Stella lying in the bubbly-filled tub.

"What the hell, Miles?"

I took a seat on the toilet.

"What is wrong with you? Are you really mad that I didn't attend your friend's wedding with you?"

"I'm just tired."

This was the first time I'd seen her like this since I'd met her.

"Enjoy your bath," I said as I walked out of the bathroom.

Taking a seat on her bed, I picked up one of her psychology books and looked at it. As I was reading a few pages, Stella walked into the bedroom wrapped in a towel and looked at me.

"What are you doing?"

"I'm just looking at your books." I smiled, shutting the book and setting it to the side. "Come here and lay down on your stomach."

"Why?" Her brows furrowed. "I'm not in the mood tonight."

"I wasn't talking about sex, Stella. I'm giving you a nice massage to help you relax." A smile crossed my lips.

"The towel stays on, Miles."

"I know. Come on. Lie down."

She climbed onto the bed, laid on her stomach, and I began massaging her, starting with her shoulders.

"Oh, God. That feels so good," she moaned.

As much as I tried to control my cock from getting hard, I

couldn't. Massaging her excited me, especially how much I knew she enjoyed it. I reached around, undid her towel, and moved it down, covering her beautiful ass. I needed access to her entire back. My hands moved across her back as my fingers massaged every inch. I stared at her as her eyes closed, and she fell asleep. Grabbing a blanket, I covered her with it, walked out of the room, and took care of my hard cock that ached for her.

I poured myself a bourbon and took it to the rooftop, where I could stare out at the brightly lit city. Thoughts about Stella swirled around in my head. I cared about her, maybe a little too much, which concerned me.

CHAPTER 17

Stella

I awoke, covered in a throw blanket, with the towel still on me. It was three a.m., and I couldn't believe I'd fallen asleep while Miles was giving me a massage. That was a lie. He had me so relaxed that I couldn't help it. The way his strong hands moved across my back and how his fingers dug into me was total bliss.

I got up, put on a nightshirt, pulled back the covers, and fell back asleep.

The following morning, I flew out of bed and ran into the bathroom.

"Oh, come on," I said. "What the hell is going on?"

I heard footsteps behind me. Miles took hold of my hair and held it back.

"I see it's not a good morning. It appears you have the flu."

"I guess so." I vomited one more time and was humiliated that he saw me like this.

He grabbed a tissue and handed it to me. Wiping my mouth, I threw the tissue in the toilet, flushed, and stood up.

"You need to get back in bed. Is there anything I can get you?" he asked.

"No. I'll be okay. I feel better now."

"I'll have Dora make you some toast," he said, walking out of the room.

Putting on my robe, I went into the kitchen.

"Good morning, Stella," Dora said. "Your toast will be right up. Can I make you a cup of coffee or tea?"

"I'll have some peppermint tea. Thank you, Dora."

I sat at the island next to Miles while he ate his scrambled eggs and read the news on his phone.

"Thanks for the massage last night. I really enjoyed it."

"You're welcome. You were out pretty fast."

"You relaxed me to the point of no return." I smirked.

The corners of his mouth lifted into a handsome smile. "Anytime you need a massage, just ask. I have to get to the office. I'll see you tonight." He left the kitchen.

Dora set my toast and tea down in front of me.

"I have to get to the grocery store before it gets busy. Is there anything else you want me to pick up for you?" she asked.

"No. I'm fine. Thanks, Dora."

I picked up my phone and took a bite of my toast. Looking at the date, something occurred to me. Opening my period app showed that I should have already started. Suddenly, my belly twisted, and I felt sick again. My heart started racing as I began to sweat.

"Nope. I'm not pregnant." I shook my head. "I'm sick. I have the flu, and that's why I'm late." I tried to convince myself, but somehow I knew better.

I immediately called Jordyn.

"Hey, you," she answered. "I'm on my way into a meeting. Can I call you back?"

"I think I'm pregnant," I blurted out.

"Stella, are you serious?"

"My period was due two weeks ago."

"And you're just now figuring that out?" she asked.

"It's been crazy here finishing up my other classes, starting my new ones, getting married, and moving into the penthouse. I honestly didn't think about it. Besides, remember how my pills were screwed up?"

"Yeah, I remember. Shit. What are you going to do?"

"I don't know. I guess I'll go get a pregnancy test and find out. Please pray for me that it's negative."

"I'm praying hard. I just got to my meeting. I'll call you later."

After I showered and dressed, I stepped out of the building and walked two blocks to the drug store. Standing in the aisle, looking at the different pregnancy tests, I placed my hand on my belly as the feeling of nausea intensified. I grabbed the Clearblue box with two test sticks inside. One test stick spelled out the words pregnant and not pregnant, while the other was a plus or minus sign for double accuracy. At least that's what the box said. Taking a deep breath, I walked up to the counter, paid, and returned to the penthouse. Going into the bathroom, I took the test sticks out of the box. I could feel my body trembling at the possibility I could be pregnant. After peeing on the sticks, I set them down, washed my hands, set the time on my phone, and sat on the floor against the bathtub, hugging my knees.

"Oh! Stella, I didn't know you were home," Dora walked into the bathroom with a stack of towels, looked at the sticks on the counter, and stared at me.

"I didn't know you were here, either."

"I was in the laundry room doing laundry. Are you okay?" She put the towels away in the cabinet.

"I don't know yet." Tears filled my eyes.

"Oh, sweetie." She sat on the floor and placed her arm around me. "It'll be okay." She hugged me as I placed my head on her shoulder.

"No, it won't. Miles doesn't like kids under the age of ten. He said he never wants children."

"He also never wanted a wife, and now look," she said.

"You know it's not a real marriage, Dora. He only married me to get his company."

The timer on my phone went off, and I felt like I was going to be sick. This could possibly be my biggest life-changing event, and I wasn't ready to face it. I slowly got up from the floor and stared at the two test sticks. One said "Pregnant," and the other displayed a dark blue plus sign.

"Oh, God." I cupped my hand over my mouth as tears streamed down my face.

"Oh, Stella. It'll be okay." Dora hugged me. "Look at me." She broke our embrace and held my shoulders. "I haven't known you very long, but I already know what a strong woman you are. Miles, on the other hand, needs some therapy." She smirked.

I let out a light laugh.

"You, my darling, will not be alone in this. I will help you in any way I can. You're having a baby." She smiled. "Nothing else in this world is God's greatest gift. You were blessed. Remember that."

"I know. How am I going to tell Miles? He's going to be so pissed. This changes everything, Dora."

"He may be a little upset at first, but he'll come to terms with it. He seems to be handling the marriage just fine."

"Right." I shook my head. "He doesn't even let me sleep in his bed after sex."

"Well, he's an idiot. The last thing you need is stress. It's not good for you or the baby. You have eleven months left of this so-called marriage, and the baby will be born in what—seven months?"

"I don't know how far along I am."

"Doesn't matter. It will be before your marriage contract is up. He has no choice but to be a father to that child. I'll get rid of the evidence for you." She scooped up the test sticks and the box and took them with her.

After we sat on the bed and talked a while longer, she left for the day. I didn't know how the hell I was going to tell him I was pregnant with his baby. First, I needed to call my OB/GYN and get in as soon as possible. Picking up my phone, I called the office.

"Dr. Gregario's office. Belinda speaking. How can I help you?"

"Hi, Belinda. This is Stella Harper. I need to make an appointment."

"And what will you be coming in for?"

"I just took a pregnancy test, and it's positive. Actually, I took two."

"Congratulations, Stella. Let me see when I can get you an appointment. Dr. Gregario had a cancellation for this Friday at one o'clock. Will that work?"

"Friday at one is fine. Thank you."

"Great. You're all set, and we'll see you Friday."

Miles

I'd just returned from a meeting and sat behind my desk. Pulling my phone from my pocket, I texted Stella to see how she was feeling.

"How are you feeling?"

"A little better."

"I hope you're resting."

"I'm doing homework that's due tomorrow. So yeah, I'm resting."

"I wouldn't call that resting, Stella. But I understand that you need to finish your homework. I'll be a little late tonight. I have a dinner meeting at six o'clock."

"Okay. I'll see you later."

My office door opened, and Uncle Ben walked in.

"I haven't seen you the past couple of days," he said, taking a seat in front of my desk.

"I've been busy working."

"The Schmidt deal fell through," he said.

"What? Why?" I spoke with anger.

"They didn't like our terms."

"What are you talking about? Peter was fine with the terms at our last meeting."

"I changed them. I didn't feel the terms were right."

I sat there with a stern look, shaking my head. "Those terms were fine." I pointed at him. "What the fuck are you doing, Uncle Ben?"

"I'm overseeing this company and making sure we don't make deals that will cost us money. The Schmidt deal would have cost us."

"Only for the first six months. Do you not look at the bigger picture?"

"I do look at the bigger picture, and the bigger picture was telling me it was not a good investment." He stood up. "I just wanted to let you know. If you have a problem with it, tell the boss. Oh, wait. That's me. Too bad if you don't like it. I make the final decisions around here."

He walked out of my office. Picking up a pen, I threw it across the room.

"Fuck!" I shouted.

The door opened, and Isla walked in. "Are you okay?"

"No!" I shouted. "I'm sorry. I didn't mean to shout at you. That man." I shook my finger. "Eleven months can't come fast enough."

"Is that all you can think about?" she asked.

"Uh, yeah." I narrowed my eyes. "What else would I be thinking about?"

"Oh, I don't know. Perhaps your wife and how the divorce will affect her?" Her brow arched.

"Stella is a strong woman. She'll be fine."

"If you so, boss." She turned, walked out of my office, and shut the door.

I met Leonard Hathaway and his brother, Jacob, at Daniel. It was a good business meeting, and I was more than happy to help his company.

"I'll be in touch." I shook both their hands.

I was supposed to run every proposal and deal by my uncle, but he wasn't getting his hands on this one.

CHAPTER 18

Miles

 I stepped into the foyer of the penthouse, set my briefcase down, and poured myself a bourbon. Looking around, I didn't see Stella, so I went to her room and lightly knocked on the door.

"Come in."

"I wasn't sure if you'd be sleeping. It's late," I said, walking in and sitting on the edge of her bed.

"I'm almost done with this paper. How was your dinner meeting?"

"It was good. My uncle shot down a deal that I made today. He didn't feel like it was good."

"And you disagree?" she asked.

"One hundred percent. I need to take over that company before he runs it into the ground."

"There's nothing you can do right now, Miles."

"I know." I brought my hand up and softly stroked her cheek.

"Come to my room when you're finished with your paper."

"I'm really tired tonight."

"I didn't say we had to have sex. Maybe I just want some company tonight."

"You never want me to stay in your bed. What's going on?" she cocked her head.

"Nothing is going on. Tonight, I want you there. Is that so much to ask?"

"No. I'll be there in a few minutes," she said.

"Thank you." I stood up from the bed, headed to my room, changed into pajama bottoms, and climbed into bed.

It wasn't that I never wanted her to stay. I did. But I had my reasons for why I always asked her to leave after sex. Tonight was different. After the shit day I had, I didn't want to be alone, and somehow, I knew that having her in my bed all night would help ease the pain and stress I felt.

A few moments later, the door opened, and Stella walked in. She looked exhausted but still as beautiful as always. She climbed in next to me as I held out my arm. Her body snuggled against mine, and I held her tight while her head rested on my chest.

"Goodnight, Stella."

"Goodnight, Miles," she softly whispered.

~

*S*tella

I woke up and looked at the clock. It was five-thirty a.m. His alarm would go off in half an hour, and I needed to make my escape as I felt the vomit rise in my throat. Carefully climbing out of bed, I quietly left his bedroom and ran to my bathroom, locking the door and turning on the shower so he didn't hear me vomiting. I didn't know when or how I would tell him about the baby.

After turning off the shower, I heard a knock at the door. Shit.

"Hold on." I quickly took off my sleep shirt and wrapped a large towel around me. Opening the door, I smiled. "Good morning."

"Morning. I woke up, and you were gone. Why was the door locked?"

"Habit, I guess. I woke up early and couldn't sleep. I didn't want to wake you, so I thought I'd take a quick shower and get ready for class."

"I see. I'm going to take a shower and get ready for work. How are you feeling?"

"Better," I lied.

"Good. I'll see you at breakfast." He walked away.

I placed my hand on my belly. There was a tender side to him last night—a part of him I knew existed, but he rarely showed. The scars of his past held him prisoner, and I needed to find the key and set him free.

After getting dressed, I went to the kitchen. Miles glanced up at me from his phone as he sat at the table.

"Morning, Stella. Tea?" Dora asked.

"Morning, Dora. Thank you."

"What is with you and tea lately?" Miles asked as I sat down across from him.

"I like tea. I go through a tea phase every once in a while." I smiled, staring at him, remembering how his strong arms held me all night.

He stood up from his chair. "I have to get to the office." He walked over and kissed the top of my head. "I'll see you later."

"Have a good day," I said.

"You too. Have fun in school." He winked with a smile.

My second class ended early. When Sean picked me up, I

had him take me to Starbucks. Even though I was tired as hell, I craved an iced coffee.

"You can go," I said to him as he opened the car door for me. "I'm going to walk around and do a little shopping."

"Call me when you're ready to be picked up." He smiled.

"I can take a cab home."

"I don't think Miles would like that, Stella."

"Miles doesn't have to know, does he?" A smirk crossed my lips as I patted his chest.

I walked down the street, sipping my decaf iced coffee, when I ran into Uncle Ben.

"Ben," I said.

"Stella, what a nice surprise." He smiled. "How's married life?"

"It's amazing," I lied.

He glanced at his watch. "I have some time before I have to get to a meeting around the corner. Let's sit and talk for a bit."

"Sure," I spoke nervously.

We crossed the street and took a seat on a bench.

"You're a smart girl, Stella. For goodness sake, you're a psychologist. You have to see the issues with Miles."

"I don't know what you're talking about, Ben."

"You do know what I'm talking about. Your marriage to my nephew is fake. I'm not stupid. He married you to gain control of Bradshaw Capital. How does he treat you?"

"He treats me good."

"It's Impossible. Miles doesn't know how to be in a relationship. The man has a heart of stone, and you're going to get hurt. The only life he knows how to live is the business life. That's his life—it always has been—and you won't change that. I saw the way you looked at him at dinner that night. You're in love with him."

"Of course I am. If I weren't, I never would have married him." I sipped my coffee.

"Don't bullshit me, Stella. You're a nice girl, and Miles will hurt you. You don't deserve that. Think about what you're doing. You would be smart to get out of this marriage now and save yourself the heartache and pain that will come."

"You want me to end my marriage so Miles can't gain control of his company. You don't care about me or my feelings, Ben."

He stood up and stared at me. "I do care, Stella. You're a pawn in his game. A game that will ultimately destroy you. You may walk away a rich woman, but your heart and self-worth will suffer. I have to get to my meeting." He walked away.

I sighed, bringing the cup to my lips.

I had an Uber pick me up and take me to Bradshaw Capital. I'd never been there and wanted to see where Miles worked. Would he be pissed that I just showed up? Yeah, probably, but I didn't care.

I took the elevator up to the forty-second floor. When I stepped out, I asked the gentleman sitting behind the large cherry desk where Miles' office was. When I reached his office, a woman with short dark hair greeted me.

"How can I help you?"

"Is Miles in there?" I pointed to his office.

"And you are?" Her brows furrowed.

"His wife, Stella."

"Oh my gosh." She grinned, stood up, and hugged me. "I'm so happy to finally meet you. I'm Isla, his secretary, assistant, and slave." She laughed.

"It's nice to meet you, Isla."

She walked over to his door and slowly opened it.

"Miles, someone is here to see you," she said.

"Who?" I heard him ask.

"Me." I stepped inside his office.

"Stella, what are you doing here?" His brows furrowed.

Isla shut the door behind me.

"I was in the area and wanted to see where you spend your days and late nights."

"Shouldn't you be in class?"

"Classes are over. This is nice." I looked around his oversized office.

"Thank you." He glanced at his watch. "I have a meeting in the conference room in five minutes. I wish you had called first."

"No big deal. I just wanted to see where you worked. Like I said, I was in the area."

"Did Sean drive you here?"

"No. I took an Uber. I had Sean take me to Starbucks after class and then told him he could leave. I wanted to do some shopping, but I ended up sitting in a park for a while."

"Why?" His brows furrowed.

"I guess to relax and enjoy my iced coffee."

A small smile framed his lips as he walked over and kissed my forehead.

"I have to get to my meeting. I'll see you tonight."

"Okay." We walked out of his office together.

"Isla, I'll be in conference room two," he told her.

"It was nice to meet you, Isla." I smiled.

"You too, Stella. We should do lunch sometime."

"I'd like that."

CHAPTER 19

Miles

"She's a beautiful woman," Isla said, following me into my office.

"If you're talking about Stella, yes, she is." I sat behind my desk.

"I can see why you chose her to be your wife."

"She's not only beautiful, but she's smart."

"Is she?" Isla's brow arched.

"She is." I smirked. "She married me, didn't she?"

Isla shook her head, walked out of my office, and shut the door.

Stella showing up at my office unannounced didn't sit well with me. She should have called and told me she was coming. I hated surprises, and maybe I needed to tell her that.

I left the office around eight p.m. When I stepped off the elevator and made my way into the living room, I stopped when I saw her lying on the couch, sleeping, with an open textbook on her chest. Picking up the textbook, I set it on the coffee table. Her eyes opened, and she stared at me.

"Hey, sleepyhead." I smiled.

"What time is it?" She sat up.

"It's eight-thirty. I just got home."

"Shit." She placed her hand on her forehead. "I don't remember closing my eyes."

"You've been awfully tired the last week," I said. "You say you feel okay, but I don't think you do. Maybe you should go see a doctor."

"I'm fine, Miles. These two new classes are kicking my ass. That's all."

"Did you eat dinner?" I asked.

"Not really."

"How about I order us a pizza?"

"Okay. That sounds good." A small smile framed her lips.

I went to my room, called the pizza place, and changed into a pair of dark gray sweatpants and a T-shirt. When the pizza arrived, I set the box down on the island along with the bag of breadsticks and an antipasto salad.

"There's something I need to tell you," I said, pouring a glass of bourbon.

"And what do you have to tell me, Mr. Bradshaw?" Stella asked with a smirk as she took down two plates from the cabinet.

"First, can I pour you a glass of wine?" I grabbed the bottle.

"Uh, no. I don't like to drink wine with pizza."

"Okay. What do you want then?"

"Just a bottle of water is fine." She smiled. "So, spit it out. What do you have to tell me?" She sat at the table.

"I don't like surprises. I never have." I handed her the bottle of water and took my seat across from her.

"Okay?" Her brows furrowed. "Care to elaborate?"

"You showing up at my office unannounced was a surprise. You should have called me first."

She bit into her pizza as she stared at me from across the table.

"So I surprised you at the office, and you didn't like it?"

"Yes."

"My intention wasn't to surprise you. I just wanted to see where you worked."

"You didn't call. You didn't text. You just showed up unannounced and caught me off guard. Next time, if you feel the need to come to the office, let me know before you just show up."

Her eyes steadily narrowed. "Okay then. No more surprises. But let me ask you this. What is your problem with surprises?"

Stella

I already knew what his problem was, but I wanted to hear him say it.

"I just don't like them," he said, plating his salad.

"It's because you fear losing control, right?"

"Don't be ridiculous, Stella."

"Well, I guess I'm not surprised because surprises are for mentally stable people."

"Excuse me?" His brow arched.

"Unexpected situations, such as surprises, cause you stress because you need to be in control of every situation at all times. If you know what to expect, your brain can keep you out of harm's way. But a surprise takes your anxiety to a whole other level."

"Wow. Are you seriously shrinking me right now? And I don't have anxiety." He pointed at me with a stern look.

"I'm just explaining to you why you don't like surprises, just in case you wanted to know."

"You basically said I was mentally unstable." His eyes narrowed.

"I did, didn't I? I'm sorry. What I meant to say was that you're sensory sensitive."

"Okay. Enough." He stood up from his chair and took his plate to the sink. He turned and looked at me. "You will never shrink me again, understand?"

"Okay. I won't shrink you again. But if the occasion—"

"Stella, enough." He cut me off.

I pursed my lips and made the zipping motion. He walked over, grabbed my hand, and stood me up from my chair, his face mere inches from mine.

"I don't like you shrinking me." His lips softly brushed against mine. "But I do like you in my bed." He had me in his arms in one swoop, carrying me to his bedroom.

Our night of passion overtook me like it always did. He thrust in and out of me slowly, his lips softly caressing mine before moving down to my breasts. His mouth wrapped around my hardened peaks, which intensified the pleasurable bliss I was already lost in. He hit all the right spots, and my second orgasm of the evening erupted. Hard moans escaped me as my body shook.

"God, Stella. The things you do to me," he moaned, halting and exploding inside me.

His body dropped on mine, and my arms wrapped tightly around him. It took a while for our breathing to return to normal. For a few moments, I forgot I was pregnant. This was supposed to be one of the happiest times of my life, but it was one I feared the most.

He rolled off me. His gaze caught my attention.

"That was incredible." The corners of his mouth curved up.

"It always is." I lay my head on his chest.

"You're welcome to stay in my bed again tonight. I know you're exhausted."

"Thank you." My lips pressed against his muscular chest.

Miles

Holding her in my arms felt like I was losing control. I had to fight the feelings trying to escape the box I had neatly wrapped up in my mind.

My alarm went off, and she was gone when I opened my eyes. Sighing, I climbed out of bed and took a shower. Stella strolled in as I was making a cup of coffee in the kitchen.

"Good morning," she said.

"You were gone again," I spoke sternly.

"I took a shower." She grabbed the tea kettle and filled it with water.

"Couldn't sleep?" I asked. "Maybe you need to go see a doctor about that."

"Can I make you some breakfast since Dora is off today?" she asked, reaching into the cabinet and grabbing the box of tea.

"No." I took my coffee to the island. My phone rang. Glancing at it, I saw my aunt calling.

"Hello."

"Miles, I'm at the hospital. Ben had a stroke," she cried.

"I'm on my way, Aunt Gabby."

"What's wrong?" Stella asked.

"My Uncle Ben had a stroke. I'll talk to you later." I took

the elevator down to the lobby and hailed a cab. Pulling out my phone, I texted Sean.

"No need to pick me up at the penthouse. I'm on my way to the hospital. My uncle had a stroke. Meet me there."

"I will, Miles. Hope everything's okay."

When I reached the hospital, I took the elevator to the room where they kept my uncle. When I walked in, my Aunt Gabby hugged me.

"Thank you for coming." Tears filled her eyes.

"How is he?" I asked, staring at my uncle as he slept.

She shook her head and sat in the chair beside his bed.

"It's not good, Miles. His speech is impaired, and the left side of his body is paralyzed."

The doctor walked in and spoke to both of us about my uncle's condition.

"And how long until he can return to work?" I asked.

"At this time, we don't know. Due to the severity of his stroke, we're looking at many months, a year, or if ever. He's going to need a lot of rehabilitation."

When I left the hospital, I pulled my phone from my pocket and called Isla.

"Hello, Miles."

"Isla, I want you to call the board members for an emergency board meeting. Also, call Nolan and get him to my office."

"Will do, Miles."

Walking into my office, I set my briefcase down.

"The board members are on their way. What is going on?" Isla asked.

"My uncle suffered a stroke."

"Oh my gosh. Is he okay?"

"He's alive, but as far as being okay, no. I need a cup of coffee before I head to the board room."

After Isla handed me my coffee, I entered the board room, where the board members sat, waiting for me.

"What's this about, Miles?" Gary, one of the members, asked.

"Ben has had a stroke and will no longer be able to fulfill his position as this company's CEO and Chairman of the board, as my mother appointed him after her death. I will be taking over the company that is rightfully mine."

"Your mother stipulated in her will that you will not take over until you've been married for a full year," Gary said.

I glanced at Nolan.

"If Ben can no longer serve as chairman and CEO of Bradshaw Capital, the company's president shall step in and take over. The company is his, and rightfully so."

"And how do you know that Ben won't be back before your year is up?" Robert, one of the board members, asked.

"His doctor told me it could be months or even a year, if ever. I know you've all been on this board for many years and always stood behind my parent's decisions. But they aren't here anymore. I am. And if you don't like it, I suggest you remove yourselves from the board. This is my company, and I'm running it as I see fit. Have a good day." I walked out of the boardroom before they could say another word, and Nolan followed.

"I think it's time for a fresh board of directors." I glanced at him.

CHAPTER 20

Stella

"You're six weeks pregnant, Stella." Dr. Gregario smiled. "I'm going to send in a script for prenatal vitamins, and I want you to start taking them immediately. In the meantime, I'll have my nurse come in and take you to the ultrasound room."

"An ultrasound already?" I asked.

"I want to make sure everything is okay. Hang tight."

As I sat on the table, swinging my legs back and forth, waiting for the nurse to walk in, my phone dinged with a text from Miles.

"I'm taking you out tonight. Be ready around seven o'clock."

My brows furrowed.

"Why?"

"Because we have celebrating to do. I'll talk to you later."

I prayed to God we weren't celebrating his uncle's death. Shit. I knew Miles had issues, but that would be fucked up. I had to know.

"Please tell me your uncle didn't pass away."

"No. He didn't. I'll explain everything to you later."

I let out a sigh of relief. The nurse walked in and led me to the ultrasound room. Lying on the table, Dr. Gregario performed the ultrasound.

"See this little sac right here?" He pointed to the screen. "That's your baby."

Tears filled my eyes as I stared at the tiny human developing inside me.

"Everything looks good, Stella. I want to see you in four weeks. You'll begin monthly visits until you're twenty-eight weeks. Take your vitamins, eat well, and no stress."

No stress. Right. My stress level was at an all-time high, knowing I had to tell Miles he was going to be a father.

"Thank you, Dr. Gregario. I'll see you next month."

When I arrived back at the penthouse, I called Jordyn, praying she would answer.

"I was just going to call you," she answered.

"Great minds think alike." I smiled.

"How did your doctor's appointment go?"

"It went well. I'm six weeks pregnant. Dr. Gregario did an ultrasound and said everything looks good."

"Yay! I'm so happy for you. When are you telling Miles?"

"I don't know. He's taking me out to celebrate tonight."

"Celebrate what?"

"I'm not sure. All he said was to be ready at seven o'clock. He's going to suspect something when I won't drink alcohol."

"Then you have no choice but to tell him tonight," Jordyn said. "You can't keep this from him any longer, Stella. It's too much stress on you and the baby."

"I know." I sighed. "I'm going to take a nap. If I don't, I'll never make it tonight."

"Okay. Get some rest. Call me tomorrow."

"I will. Bye, Jordyn."

If there ever was a time I needed my best friend here in New York, it was now. I lay down and slept for two hours. The exhaustion that overtook me was unbearable. When I awoke, I studied and got ready for when Miles came home. My phone dinged with a text. Picking it up, I saw a text from Miles.

"I'm running late, so Sean will pick you up and bring you to the restaurant."

"Okay. See you soon."

I shook my head.

The elevator dinged, and Sean stepped into the foyer.

"Good evening, Stella. You look beautiful."

"Thanks, Sean." I smiled.

I climbed into the back of the Escalade. Sean shut the door and climbed into the driver's seat.

"Where am I meeting Miles?" I asked.

"Per Se."

I inhaled a breath as I stared out the window. When Sean pulled up to the restaurant, Miles was standing outside waiting. He opened the door and extended his hand.

"You look beautiful." A handsome grin crossed his lips.

"Thank you."

We walked into the restaurant and were immediately seated. The waiter walked over to our table and poured water into our glasses.

"Good evening, Mr. Bradshaw. It's good to see you again."

"Good evening, Paul. I'll have a bourbon, neat."

"And for the lovely lady?" Paul smiled, looking at me.

"I'm just going to stick with water."

As soon as Paul walked away, Miles narrowed his eyes at me.

"You're not drinking?" he asked.

"My stomach has been bothering me all day."

"Again? You really need to see a doctor, Stella. This has been going on long enough."

"I know." I picked up my water glass.

"We're here to celebrate, and you're not ordering a drink."

"What are we celebrating?" I asked.

"Bradshaw Capital is officially mine. You're looking at the new Chairman and CEO." He grinned.

"Congratulations, Miles. How?"

"Unfortunately, my uncle is incapacitated and will not be back to work for a period of time, if ever."

"I'm sorry to hear that." I looked down. "I hope you're not happy about his condition."

"No, I'm not." He sighed. "I truly hope he recovers."

Paul approached our table with the bourbon for Miles and took our dinner order.

"Now that you got your company, what about us?"

"That's what I want to talk to you about," he said, and suddenly, I felt sick again. "We no longer have to be married, so I'm having my attorney draw up the annulment papers. We can sign as soon as they're ready, and our marriage will be dissolved as if it never happened."

My heart started racing, and I fought to hold back the tears.

"I will still give you the other half of the money. With that, you can afford a really nice apartment and still go to school full-time for your doctorate."

Oh God. The tears were forcing their way through.

"I know it will take you time to find a place, and my realtor is looking as we speak. I gave him your number, so he'll call you."

Not only did I feel humiliated, but I also felt an anger that I'd never felt before. I needed to remain in control.

"Okay." I forced a smile. "You are over the moon about your company. Look at you. I don't think I've ever seen you this happy."

"I am, Stella." He smiled, sipping his bourbon. "It's what I've worked so hard for. You'll understand that when you get your doctorate."

"Yeah. I suppose I will."

We finished dinner and left the restaurant. As soon as we stepped into the penthouse, I set my purse down on the island and kicked off the heels that were killing my feet.

"Let's go finish celebrating in the bedroom." Miles smiled.

"As much as I'd love to, I'm really tired and not feeling well." I bent down to pick up my shoes and accidentally knocked my purse off the island. Some of the contents fell out, including the ultrasound picture Dr. Gregario gave me.

"Shit," I said, bending down.

"Let me help you." Miles picked up the ultrasound picture and stared at it. "What's this?" His eyes stared into mine. "This looks like—"

I stared at him as terror coursed through me.

"I'm pregnant, Miles."

CHAPTER 21

Miles

I froze when I heard those words come from her mouth. My heart started racing, and I broke out into a sweat.

"Is it mine?" I stood up.

"Of course, it's yours." Her brows furrowed. "How can you even ask me that? I'm six weeks along."

"How long have you known?" I asked sternly.

"Just a few days. I saw my doctor this afternoon."

"And when were you planning on telling me?"

"Tonight, tomorrow, hell, I don't know." She threw her hands up in the air. "I know how you feel about children."

"Are you keeping it?"

"Yes, I'm keeping it!" she shouted.

"Did you do this on purpose to trap me?"

"No! It was an accident."

"I don't want children, Stella. I already told you that. My work takes up ninety-nine percent of my life, and that's what I need to focus on. When I come home, I want to relax, not come home to a baby's drama. The crying, sleepless nights, toys everywhere, illnesses, having to pretend to be something I'm not."

"That's okay, Miles. You don't have to pretend because you won't ever be a part of my baby's life or mine! You were manipulated and emotionally abandoned your whole life. And the last thing I want is for my child to suffer the same thing. Tell your attorney to step it up and get those annulment papers ready so I can be out of your life as soon as possible." She grabbed her purse and stormed out of the kitchen. I followed her to the elevator.

"Where are you going?" I gripped her arm.

"That is none of your business. You do you, and I do me. Remember?" She jerked out of my grip and stepped into the elevator.

I ran my hand down my face, walked over to the bar, and poured a drink. Taking it up to the rooftop, I finished it and threw the glass against the brick. What the fuck was I going to do?

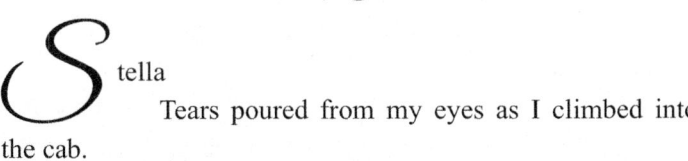

Stella

Tears poured from my eyes as I climbed into the cab.

"Where to?" the cab driver asked.

"Just take me to the New York Hilton in Midtown."

I was shaking, and my mind was filled with chaos. I couldn't stay at the penthouse tonight, and I couldn't look at him anymore. As much as I wanted to block his number, I couldn't. He needed to be able to reach me when the annulment papers were ready to be signed.

I entered the Hilton lobby and walked up to the desk.

"Good evening. Checking in?" The man behind the counter smiled.

"I don't have a reservation, but I need a room."

"For how many nights?" he asked.

"I'm not sure yet." I looked down.

"Okay. Let me check what's available. Our Urban room with one king bed is available for three nights only."

"I'll take it." I pulled out my license and credit card.

"Do you have any bags we can help you with?" he asked.

"No. I don't."

He looked at me strangely.

"I left in a hurry. I'll have my things tomorrow," I told him, even though it wasn't any of his business.

"Very well. Enjoy your stay." He handed me the keycard.

I took the elevator up to the fifteenth floor, found my room, and stepped inside. Throwing my purse and myself down on the bed, I grabbed the pillow, placed it over my face, and screamed. I'd never felt so alone as I did at that moment. Pulling my phone from my purse, I checked to see if Miles had texted me. He didn't. Asshole. Tomorrow morning, while he was at the office, I would return to the penthouse, pack my things, and leave.

After taking a hot bath to calm down, I pulled up apartments on my phone. I needed to find one as soon as possible, and I wasn't about to wait for his realtor. I could do this. I could be a single mom. Millions of women did it every day. I wasn't sure if Miles would still deposit the rest of the money in my account. After the bomb I dropped on him tonight, he probably wouldn't. He was an emotionless, broken man who only cared about himself and his needs.

Miles

Returning to the kitchen, I saw the ultrasound picture sitting on the island. Picking it up, I stared at it but couldn't make anything out. Shaking my head, I set it down and went to bed.

I was up all night, tossing and turning, worrying about Stella and where she ran off to. After showering, I walked into the kitchen.

"Good morning, Miles," Dora spoke. "Where's Stella?"

"I don't know. She left last night." I walked over to the coffee machine.

"And this?" She held up the ultrasound picture.

"What about it?"

"What happened between the two of you?" she asked.

"She's pregnant. I told her I didn't want kids, and she left. End of discussion." I walked out of the kitchen, grabbed my briefcase, and stepped onto the elevator.

I'd felt this pain in my heart since last night—a pain I couldn't describe.

"Isla, call maintenance and clear my new office immediately." I stormed past her and into my office.

"Are you planning on moving in today?" she asked.

"Yes. After they clear everything out, I want everything from my office transferred."

"I'll get on it right away, Miles."

I sat behind my desk, pulled my phone from my suit coat, and called Levi.

"Good morning, friend. To what do I own the honor?"

"I need to talk to you," I spoke sternly.

"It sounds serious."

"It is. It's very serious. When can you meet?"

"Are you available for lunch at one o'clock?" he asked.

"I'll make it happen. Where?"

"Gramercy Tavern," he said.

"I'll be there."

"Miles, are you okay?"

"Far from it. I'll see you at one o'clock."

I set my phone down and sighed.

"Isla, come in here," I shouted.

"Yes, boss?"

"I want a memo typed up and sent out telling everyone about Ben, how we wish him well, and that I am the new CEO of Bradshaw Capital."

"I'll get on it. So, where am I going if you're moving offices today?"

"You're moving desks. Tell Marissa that she's taking your desk and you're taking hers. She'll report to the new president when I decide who that shall be."

"Leaving me to be the bad guy?" Her brow arched.

"I've been the bad guy enough lately." I turned my chair around and faced the city.

CHAPTER 22

Miles

"You look like shit," Levi said as I approached the booth.

"Thanks." I slid in across from him.

"I took the liberty of ordering you a coffee, but looking at you, I think you want something stronger."

"Coffee is fine." I picked up the cup and brought it to my lips.

"What the fuck is going on, Miles?"

"Stella is pregnant."

"Oh shit." His eyes widened.

The waitress walked over and took our lunch order.

"I'll have the smoked wagyu brisket," I said, closing the menu.

"I'll have the same," Levi said. "When did this happen? Better yet, how did this happen?"

"Apparently, six weeks ago." I shook my head. "I asked her if she had done it on purpose. Of course, she denied it and said it was an accident."

"You weren't using a condom?" His brow arched.

"She's my wife and was on birth control."

"Fake wife." He pointed at me.

"She stormed out of the penthouse last night after we argued. I told her I didn't want kids, and she told me I didn't have to worry about it."

"What did she mean by that?" he asked.

"She said I've been manipulated and emotionally abandoned my whole life, and she doesn't want that for her child. Can you fucking believe that?"

"What? That she doesn't want that for her kid?"

"No. That I've been manipulated and emotionally abandoned."

"Well, she does speak the truth." He sipped his coffee. "Listen, Miles. I've known you since we were kids. Your father was never around because Bradshaw Capital was his life. The same went for your mother. And I think she realized what they'd done to you. That's why she did what she did before she passed away."

"Before I found out Stella was pregnant, I took her to dinner last night to tell her the good news about my company. I told her I would deposit the rest of the money in her account and have the annulment papers drawn up for us to sign."

"I'm going to ask you something, and I want an honest answer. You already know you can't bullshit me, Miles. Do you love her? Are you in love with her?"

"I don't know." I turned my head and stared out the window. "I don't even know what love is, Levi."

Our waitress walked over with our food and asked if we needed anything else.

"Two bourbons, neat," Levi said.

He stared at me with a sympathetic look.

"I know I think about her first thing in the morning, and

she's the last thing on my mind at night. She hadn't been feeling well, and I was concerned."

"Well, now you know why she wasn't feeling well. She's pregnant and probably has morning sickness."

I cocked my head at him. "That explains why she left my bed in the mornings before I woke up."

Our waitress brought over our bourbons and set them in front of us.

"Thank you," I said, picking up the glass.

"Listen, Miles. This is exactly what your mother and uncle were talking about. You don't know how to live life outside of your work."

"That is not true!" I threw back my bourbon.

"Yes, it is. Yeah, back in the day, we partied too much. We would go out, get drunk, pick up women, go home, get up for work, and repeat. Then I met Laurel, and she changed that for me. Your entire life, you've been in work mode. It's what your parents drilled into your head. And like I said, I think your mother realized that. You chose Stella for a reason. She wasn't just some random chick you picked up in Vegas. I saw the way your eyes lit up when she stepped onto the plane. I saw how you looked at her at the courthouse when you two married. I was happy because I said to myself that she was the one. She was the one who was going to make him happy and realize there's more to life than work. And from the bottom of my heart, I knew you wouldn't have the marriage annulled once your year was up. But I guess I was wrong since you told her last night you're having your attorney draw up the papers."

"She deserves a better man than me."

"That's for her to decide, Miles. For fuck's sake. She's carrying your baby. YOUR BABY. You must have some sort of feeling in that heart of stone. God. If Laurel told me she was pregnant, I'd be over the moon with happiness. This child is yours and the heir to Bradshaw Capital." He pointed at me.

"I can't be a father."

"Why?"

"I already failed as a husband."

"You weren't a real husband to begin with. You can make up all kinds of excuses to convince yourself that you aren't in love with her. But I know what I know and what I see." He stood up and threw some cash on the table. "Lunch is on me, friend. Figure your shit out and call me when you do." He shook his head and walked away.

Pulling out my phone, I called Nolan.

"What's up, Miles?"

"I need the annulment papers done today."

"I'm working on them now. You'll have them by the end of the day."

"Thanks, Nolan."

I left the restaurant and had Sean drive me back to Bradshaw Capital. When I passed Isla's desk, she told me my new office was ready. When I stepped inside, I sighed.

"I want the walls painted a different color and get these pictures off the wall."

"Why?" Isla asked.

"Because it reminds me too much of my mother and my uncle. Get it taken care of. Until it's done, I'll be down at my old office, and you'll be sitting at your old desk."

"Damn you, Miles," she whined. "You couldn't have said anything before everything was moved?"

"I'm heading to the art gallery to find new artwork. I'll see you tomorrow."

Pulling my phone from my pocket, I called a dear friend of mine as I sat in the back of the Escalade.

"Mr. Miles Bradshaw. Long time no talk, my friend."

"Shaun Kind. It's good to hear your voice. How are you?"

"I'm great. Living my best life here in Los Angeles. How are you?"

"I'm doing okay."

"I'm sorry to hear about your mother. My sympathies, friend."

"Thank you. I'm calling because I've taken over Bradshaw Capital and need some new blood on the board of directors."

"Looking to clean house?" he asked.

"I am. Now that the company is mine, it's time to get rid of the old and bring in the new."

"I'll be in New York next week. Let's meet up and talk," he said. "I'm very interested in helping you out."

"Excellent. I'm looking forward to seeing you, my friend."

"You too, Miles."

I walked into the art gallery and began looking around.

"Miles Bradshaw, it's been a while."

"Chloe Bennett. You look as beautiful as always." I kissed her cheek and hugged her.

"Thank you, Miles. What brings you in? Are you looking for new artwork?"

"I am. For my new office."

"We just got in a new collection I think you'll like. Follow me."

"How's Sebastian doing?"

"He's amazing as always." She grinned.

"And your parents?" I smirked.

"Crazy as always." She laughed. "Let me know if you see anything you like."

"I will. Thank you, Chloe."

I found a couple of pieces that would look perfect in my office. When I turned around, I saw Sebastian standing there, smiling.

"Sebastian." I walked over and hugged him.

"My wife told me you were here looking at art when I walked in. How are you, Miles?"

"I'm good."

"I'm sorry that Chloe and I weren't able to attend your mother's funeral. We were in Europe. You did get the flowers we sent, right?"

"I did, and they were beautiful. Thank you. I'm happy to see you. I was going to give you a call."

"You were?"

"I want to clean house. The board of directors needs some new blood."

"You want me on your board of directors?" he asked.

"I do." I smiled. "Shaun Kind is coming in next week, and we're meeting. Join us, and we can discuss it."

"I definitely will. Just shoot me a text with the time and place. By the way, Miles. Word on the street is you got married." His brow arched.

"But yet I don't see a wedding band on your finger," Chloe said.

"Yes, I did get married, but it's complicated."

"It was complicated marrying the Kensington's ex-nanny?" Sebastian's brow raised.

I sighed, rubbing the back of my neck. "I'll tell you about it next week."

"Looking forward to it." Sebastian smiled, extending his hand. "It was good seeing you, my friend."

"It was good to see you too, Sebastian. We've let too much time pass." I shook his hand.

"Bye, sweetheart. I love you." Sebastian kissed Chloe's lips.

"I love you too. See you at home." She smiled. "Do you want the artwork delivered to your office, Miles?" she asked.

"Yes, please."

Watching the two of them interact put an ache in my heart. I needed to think, so I walked to Central Park and sat on a bench in the Conservatory Gardens.

CHAPTER 23

Stella

I stepped out of the elevator, and Dora ran into the foyer.

"Come here." She hugged me. "I am so sorry for that man."

"Thanks, Dora." Tears once again filled my eyes.

"He'll come around. Just wait and see." She broke our embrace.

"It doesn't matter if he does or doesn't. I'm leaving." I walked to my bedroom to collect my things.

"No, Stella. Just hold on. Please."

"I can't." I began throwing my things in my suitcases, wiping the tears from my eyes. "I'm moving on with my life. He made it very clear that he doesn't love me and doesn't want to be a father."

"He was in shock, honey."

"I wish that were true. I mean, yes, he was in shock. But everything he said to me, he meant. His parents really did a number on him." I breathed out a laugh as I opened the dresser drawers. "And I was the stupid one for agreeing to this arrangement. It's bad enough that I'm known around New York City as the nanny thief and wannabe husband stealer. Now, I'll be known as the nanny thief, wannabe husband stealer, and the abandoned pregnant woman who only married her baby daddy for money." I sat on the edge of the bed.

"Stop that, Stella. You both were in a situation where you could help one another."

"You know," I looked down at my hands, "the moment I ran into him in that hallway in Vegas, I felt something. The moment I looked into his eyes—I don't know." I shook my head. "I can't explain it. And that unexplainable thing is why I agreed to marry him. It wasn't just for the money so I could continue my schooling."

"It's because you felt an instant connection with him," Dora said, placing her hand on mine.

"Maybe." I stood up from the bed and finished packing. "All I know is that he's not a man for my child to be around. I knew he had issues, and I knew exactly what they were and why he was behaving the way he was. But I'm not his shrink, nor do I want to be. He's happy living his life the way he is. He's married to his work and his company." I zipped up my two suitcases.

"Where are you staying?"

I looked at Dora as a soft smile crossed my lips.

"I can't tell you that. If I do, you'll tell him if he asks. I don't want to see him again. I need time to heal my heart and focus on my schooling and the baby. Please understand."

Tears filled her eyes as she stared at me. "I understand. Please, Stella, don't be a stranger. We can meet for breakfast, lunch, or dinner sometimes."

"We will do that." I smiled. "You take care, Dora. Please don't tell Miles you saw me."

"I won't." She shook her head.

I rolled my suitcases to the elevator, pushed the button, and stepped inside. When I returned to the hotel, the nice bellman brought my luggage up to my room.

"Thank you." I handed him a generous tip.

"No problem, Miss Harper. Enjoy your stay."

Pulling out my laptop, I sat on the bed and began studying for a test I had tomorrow in one of my classes. My phone rang, and Jordyn was Facetiming me. Answering it on my laptop, I smiled.

"Hi."

"How are you?" she asked, sitting behind her desk.

"I've had better days."

"I was thinking about something all night," she said. "Move to Connecticut."

"What?" I cocked my head.

"Move here with me."

"You know I can't, Jordyn. I have my classes here."

"You're almost done with your master's, and you can attend the University of Connecticut for your doctorate. I'm here and can help you with the baby."

"And where am I supposed to live while I'm attending NYU? I can't stay in a hotel for the next month."

"Try to find one of those short-term rental apartments."

"I don't know, Jordyn. I'll have to give it some thought."

"Okay. Just remember that it doesn't matter how big New York City is. You'll run into Miles at some point."

"I know." I sighed.

"I have to prep for a meeting. I'll talk to you later."

"Bye, Jordyn."

I closed my laptop, set it down, and sat there for a moment, staring at the wall. My belly rumbled. Climbing off the bed, I grabbed my purse and left the hotel. Walking a couple of blocks, I stepped into a deli for a sandwich. After placing my order, I took my food to a small table by the window. While eating my sandwich and scrolling on my phone, I looked up and saw Mrs. Kensington standing at my table, staring at me.

"Mrs. Kensington, hi."

"Hello, Stella."

"Shouldn't you be in court or something?" I asked.

"I just came from a client meeting and decided to grab a sandwich on my way back to the firm. Do you mind?" She gestured to the empty chair across from me.

"No, not at all."

"I've been meaning to call you, but time has gotten away from me. I wanted to apologize to you."

"For?" I cocked my head.

"One, for firing you, and two, for spreading mistruths about you."

I almost fell out of my chair.

"I've since retracted my statements amongst my social circle. I told them that I misspoke about you stealing from us and what I thought you'd stolen, I found. I also said that I overreacted about you wanting to sleep with my husband because the day I fired you, I was exhausted and not thinking clearly."

"I appreciate it, Mrs. Kensington."

"Please, call me Nadine. The children miss you, Stella. I won't lie. You were the best nanny we'd ever had, and it's been hard trying to find someone to fill your shoes."

"What about the nanny who works for you now?" I asked.

"Well, that girl was irresponsible, and Brandon fired her. Please come back to us."

"I'm sorry, Nadine, but I can't. I'm finishing up my master's, and I need to focus on my doctorate."

"It was just a chance I took asking you. Anyway, being Mrs. Miles Bradshaw, you don't have to worry about working." She glanced at her watch. "I have to go. Again, I'm sorry for everything that happened. Please tell Miles that we spoke today. Enjoy the rest of your lunch." She stood up and left the deli.

I sat there, furrowing my brows, wondering why she wanted me to tell Miles that we spoke. Shaking my head, I finished my sandwich and went back to the hotel.

CHAPTER 24

Miles

I stepped into the foyer of my penthouse and set my briefcase down.

"You're home early," Dora spoke.

"I'll be working from home the rest of the day." I looked around, hoping Stella was here.

"She's not here, Miles."

Walking into her bedroom, I opened the closet and saw that all her clothes and suitcases were gone.

"Where is she?" I turned and stared at Dora.

"I haven't a clue."

"You weren't here when she came to collect her things?" I narrowed my eyes.

"No. I had a few errands to run. She must have come when I was gone," she said. "I hope you're happy." She walked away.

Rubbing the back of my neck, I sat on the edge of the bed. Taking my phone from my pocket, I texted her.

"Stella, where are you?"

She didn't respond, and I wasn't surprised. As I was

changing my clothes, my phone dinged. Walking over to the bed, I picked it up and saw a text from Nolan.

"I'm on my way to your penthouse with the annulment papers."

"Okay."

Walking over to the bar, I poured myself a drink. I heard the elevator ding, so I met Nolan in the foyer.

"Come on in," I said. "Drink?"

"No, thanks. Here are the papers for you and Stella to sign. You need to get these signed quickly so I can file them with the courts. After a court date is set, you and Stella must be there and stand in front of the judge. I've listed the reasons as irreconcilable differences. If the judge gets wind that your marriage was based on fraud, you can kiss your annulment goodbye. So, you and Stella need to be on the same page as far as your stories go."

"Thanks, Nolan. I'll try to get these back to you tomorrow. I need to find her first."

"Good luck, Miles." He patted my shoulder and headed to the elevator.

Picking up my phone, I sent Stella another text.

"I have the annulment papers, which need to be signed as soon as possible. Tell me where you are, and I'll bring them to you."

My heart started racing when I saw the three dots appear on the screen.

"We can meet at the Sculptural Garden at the Museum of Modern Art in thirty minutes."

"I'm on my way."

I called Sean and told him to meet me downstairs. He dropped me off at the museum, and I went to find Stella. I saw her sitting on a bench in the Sculptural Gardens and inhaled a deep breath before approaching her.

"Hi," I said, sitting down beside her.

"Give me the papers so I can sign them and get this over with," she spoke sternly.

I pulled the papers from the manila envelope and handed her a pen.

"Where are you staying?" I asked.

"None of your business." She quickly signed the papers and handed them to me.

"Stella, I—"

"Save it, Miles." She stared straight ahead.

"We have to go to court in front of a judge after Nolan files the papers. We need to get our stories straight about why we want the marriage annulled. The judge won't grant it if he or she knows the real reason why we got married."

"Don't worry." She stood up and looked at me. "I'll tell the judge the truth—that you're not the man I thought you were, and I made a mistake."

"You knew exactly who I was when you agreed to this marriage," I said.

"Did I really?" She cocked her head. "Anyway, it doesn't matter. I'm moving on with my life, and you'll do the same. You got what you wanted, Miles. I'm just happy it happened quickly so I could get out of this marriage."

I stared into her beautiful, sad eyes. "What about the baby?"

"What about it? As I said last night, you don't have to worry about us. The two of us will be just fine, and there will be no baby drama in your life. I'll see you in court." She hooked her purse over her shoulder and walked away.

At that moment, it felt like a piece of me had died.

Stella

"Fuck him. Fuck him. Fuck him," I mumbled, walking out of the Sculptural Garden.

Tears streamed down my face as I returned to the hotel. I started the bath water, twisted up my hair, and inhaled the lavender-scented bubbles I needed to relax and calm my nerves. Placing my hand on my belly, I held it in place and closed my eyes. The dinging sound of my phone startled me. Reaching over the tub and picking it up, I saw a text from Miles. Shaking my head, I read it.

"Stella, I'm so sorry."

How I wish I could block him and be done with all of this. But we still needed to go to court. The second the judge granted the annulment, and I walked out of that courthouse, he'd never be able to contact me again. As my phone was in my hand, it rang with an unfamiliar number. I answered it.

"Hello."

"Hello, is this Stella?" a woman's voice asked.

"Yes. This is she."

"Hi, Stella. This is Grant Roman. Miles Bradshaw gave me your number and asked that I help you find an apartment."

"Thank you, Grant, but I won't be needing your services after all."

"Oh?"

"I already found an apartment," I lied.

"I understand. Well, you have my number if you need anything."

"Thank you." I ended the call and sighed.

I thought long and hard about Jordyn's plea for me to move to Connecticut. As much as I'd love to be near her again, New York was my home. I loved the city and wouldn't let Miles Bradshaw drive me out of it. I would continue attending NYU for my doctorate, graduate, get a job, and be the best mother I could. Loving Miles Bradshaw hurt me, but hating him hurt me even more.

Miles

I tucked my hands into my pants pockets, lowered my head, and walked out of the Sculptural Gardens. I texted Sean and told him I needed some time alone and that I'd text him when I needed him to pick me up. The chaos in my mind was unbearable. Between work and Stella, it was too much.

As I walked down the city streets, I saw a couple looking at an engagement ring through the window of a jewelry store.

"Let's go in and try it on. I know it'll look beautiful on you." The man smiled at his future wife as I walked by.

I stopped and turned around. "You two are getting engaged?" I asked.

"Yes, we are." The man smiled. "I already proposed, but I wanted her to pick out the ring she loved the most."

"Congratulations." I nodded.

"Thank you," the woman spoke.

I turned and continued walking. The sun hid behind the clouds, and suddenly, the small raindrops that fell onto my head turned into a downpour. A woman pushing a baby carriage rushed to the bakery where I sought shelter. I opened the door for her and motioned for her to step inside.

"Thank you so much." She smiled.

"You're welcome. How old?" I pointed to the small child in the carriage.

"She's six weeks old today," the woman spoke.

"She's cute."

"Thank you."

I ordered a coffee and a cherry Danish, taking it to a table by the window while waiting for the rain to stop.

The woman with the baby sat at the table next to me. I stared at her as she lifted the child from the carriage. She looked at me strangely. She probably thought I was a stalker.

"I apologize for staring. My wife is expecting."

"Oh. How far along is she?"

"Seven weeks now."

"Your first?" she asked.

"Yes."

"Well, she's lucky to have you by her side. This little one's father took off when I told him I was pregnant."

I swallowed hard. "I'm sorry."

"It's okay. We're better off without him in our life. Isn't that right, baby girl?" she smiled at the child. "It looks like the rain stopped. It was nice to meet you." She put the child back into the carriage.

"It was nice to meet you, too." I smiled.

My heart sank as I watched her walk out of the bakery. On my way out, I threw the rest of my coffee and Danish in the trash can. Sean pulled up, and I climbed inside the Escalade.

"Where to, Miles?" he asked.

"Just take me home."

CHAPTER 25

THREE WEEKS LATER

Stella

I had to skip class today, and when I notified my professor last night that I wouldn't be able to attend, he wanted an explanation. He had a strict policy about absences. So, I told him I had to be in court to get my marriage annulled.

I was still at the hotel but in a different room. I wasn't having any luck finding an apartment with which I was in love. Maybe I was being too picky, but I knew what I wanted for my baby and me and in which area.

My belly was twisted in knots as I gripped my purse strap and walked up the stairs to the courthouse. I swallowed hard when I saw Miles standing there.

"Hello, Stella."

"Miles." I nodded and kept walking.

He and Nolan followed behind.

"Stella, wait. How are you?"

"I'm great, Miles." I smiled. "I'd ask how you are, but I don't care."

Nolan led us to the courtroom, where we took our seats and waited for the judge to call our names.

"In the case of Bradshaw vs. Bradshaw. Will you step up?"

Nolan, Miles, and I stepped up and stood before the judge.

"You've filed a petition for an annulment of your marriage, correct?"

"Yes, your honor," Miles and I spoke at the same time.

"The reason for the annulment is irreconcilable differences?"

"Yes, your honor," we both spoke.

"You've been married a little over two months. Marriage takes some time to get used to." The judge smiled. "Are you sure you both really want this?"

"Yes, your honor," I spoke up. "He is not the man I thought he was."

"Care to elaborate on that, Mrs. Bradshaw?"

Fuck.

"He's married to his work. That is the only priority in his life, and it always will be. He can't help it, though. It was how he was raised. I thought maybe things would be different when we got married, but they weren't. It's who he is, and unfortunately, I can't live with a man like that."

"Mr. Bradshaw?" The judge looked at him.

"She's right. Everything she said is true." He looked down.

"Petition granted. I will sign the decree, and your marriage will be annulled."

"Thank you, your honor," Nolan spoke. "Let's go." He motioned for Miles and me to leave the courtroom.

Miles

I swallowed the lump in my throat as we left the courthouse. Stella walked a few feet ahead of Nolan and me, and I needed to speak with her.

"Stella, wait."

She stopped and turned around, facing me with her sad eyes.

"We need to talk," I said.

"There's nothing to say, Miles. We're free from each other now. Please leave me alone. I have a doctor's appointment to get to."

"For the baby?" I asked.

"Yes. I have to go." She walked away.

"Can I come with you?" I shouted. She stopped, and I ran over to her. "I am the baby's father and should be there."

"You're a sperm donor." She looked down at the ground.

"That's not fair, Stella. I want to go with you."

"Don't you have to get to the office?"

"Work can wait. Please."

"Whatever, Miles."

"Sean will drive us. Come on. He's parked over here." I led her to the Escalade and opened the door.

"It's good to see you, Stella." Sean smiled.

"It's good to see you too, Sean." She stared out the window.

The entire ride to the doctor's office was silent. I didn't expect her to say anything since our marriage was just annulled, and she hated me. But I was with her, and that's all that mattered.

We walked into the building lobby and took the elevator up to the third floor. After sitting in the waiting room for a few moments, the nurse took us back into a room.

"I don't know why you even came," Stella said, sitting on the exam table.

"Because I'm worried about you."

"Yeah, right." She breathed out a laugh. "The only person you care and worry about is yourself."

"Maybe that was true not long ago, but then I met you."

"Save it, Bradshaw." She looked away from me.

The door opened, and the doctor walked in.

"Hi, Stella. Oh, hello. I'm Dr. Gregario." He extended his hand. "And you are?"

"Miles Bradshaw, the baby's father." I shook his hand.

"Sperm donor," Stella blurted out. "And ex-husband."

"Oh, I see. How are you feeling, Stella?"

"I still have morning sickness, but it's not as bad."

"Good. It will continue to improve in the coming weeks. You're ten weeks pregnant, which means you'll get to hear your baby's heartbeat. After I do an exam, we'll get a ten-week scan and check to see how your baby is growing. Mr. Bradshaw, I need you to step out for a few moments."

"Okay." I stood up from the chair, and when I went to place my hand on Stella's before walking out, she pulled away.

I walked out of the room and waited in the hallway until Dr. Gregario was finished. My phone was vibrating non-stop with calls from the office. I sent a text to Isla.

"Is there any type of emergency?"

"No."

"I'm turning my phone off. I'll be in later."

I turned my phone off and placed it in my pocket. The room door opened, and Dr. Gregario stepped out.

"The nurse will be in soon to take you and Stella down to the ultrasound room." He placed his hand on my shoulder.

I walked into the room and looked at Stella.

"Did he say everything was okay?" I asked.

"Yep." She wouldn't look at me. "Why the sudden change, Miles?" she blurted out. "We just came from the courthouse and had our fake marriage annulled. There's no reason for you to be here."

"You're my reason, and the child you're carrying is my reason."

"Please." She shook her head.

The nurse walked in. "Are you two ready to see your baby?" She smiled.

She led us to the ultrasound room and told Stella to lie on the table.

CHAPTER 26

Stella

I was angry—angry at him for wanting to be here—but I let him come, and that was on me.

"Okay, let's take a peek at that baby," Dr. Gregario said, walking into the room.

He placed the doppler on my belly and turned up the sound.

"And here is the baby's heartbeat. Nice and strong." He smiled. "Look at that baby, all cozy and growing beautifully," Dr. Gregario said as he took some measurements.

A single tear fell from my eye as I stared at my baby. He or she had already grown so much since my last visit. Miles leaned over and kissed my forehead, catching me off guard. Dr. Gregario noticed, and a soft smile crossed his lips. I wanted to reach over and smack Miles away, but feeling his lips on my skin soothed me.

"Your baby is right on schedule and looking good. I'll see you next month," Dr. Gregario said before leaving the room. "By the way. I know I don't have to remind you that stress is bad for you and the baby, Stella."

"I know, Dr. Gregario."

"Okay. You two enjoy the rest of your day. Glenda will give you the ultrasound pictures."

Miles and I climbed into the back of the Escalade.

"Weren't you supposed to have class today?" Miles asked.

"How could I go when I had to be in court?" I cocked my head.

"Right. Sorry. My realtor called and told me that you said you didn't need his services because you already found an apartment. Is that true?"

"Yeah. It is. I can do things on my own, Miles. I don't need your help with anything."

"Where are you living?"

"I'm not telling you that. Sean, can you please drop me off at that Starbucks up there? I have a couple of things to do in this area, and I need an iced coffee."

"Of course, Stella."

Sean pulled over, and Miles climbed out first to let me out. As I went to walk away, he grabbed hold of my hand.

"This isn't the end, Stella."

I stared at him, pulled out of his grip, and walked down the street.

~

Miles

I climbed back into the Escalade.

"Drop me off around the corner. I'll catch a cab to the office. I want you to follow her today and find out where she's living."

"Really, Miles?" Sean said.

"Yes, really, Sean." I arched my brow. "Report back to me later."

He did as I asked, and I hailed a cab to the office. As I walked into my new office, I smiled. It was finally completed and exactly the way I envisioned it—light true gray walls with a dark gray wall accent where a curvature couch sat, a modern glass coffee table in front, and two matching chairs on each side.

"Nice color." Isla smiled. "I love it."

"My mother hated the color gray. In fact, she despised it." I smirked, sitting in my new high-end leather executive chair behind my new desk. I pulled out the sonogram picture from my suit coat pocket.

"I need you to get me a frame for this. Something that matches my office." I handed Isla the picture.

"Baby Bradshaw." She smiled, staring at my child. "How did you get this? I can't imagine Stella just handing it over to you, especially since your marriage was annulled this morning."

"I went with her to her doctor's appointment after court."

"She let you?" Her brow arched.

"Not really. I didn't give her a choice."

"So, what's going on, Miles? You want to play daddy now?"

"Isla, I don't need your smartass remarks. Not today. I'm taking things one day at a time."

"Okay, boss. If you say so. If you need me, I'll be sitting out there at my beautiful new desk with a smile on my face."

"No, you will leave the office, go to the store, and get me a frame for my baby's picture. Make a note of the size and put it in your phone. You're not taking it with you."

"Now?" Her brows furrowed.

"Yes, now. And while you're out, grab me a corned beef

sandwich with extra swiss on an onion roll from the deli down the street." I reached into my pocket, pulled out my wallet, and handed her a one-hundred-dollar bill. "Get yourself something, too, and keep the change."

"Damn." She grinned, grabbing the hundred from my hand. "What has gotten into you?" She strutted out of my office.

I picked up my phone, turned my chair around, and called Levi. My brows furrowed when I heard a ringing phone.

"Calling me, are you?"

Turning my chair around, I smiled when I saw Levi standing in my office doorway.

"I'm digging this new look, Mr. Hotshot CEO." He grinned.

"Step into my humble office, my friend." I stood up and hugged him.

"You get your shit together yet?" His brow arched.

"I'm getting there." I smirked. "Can I pour you a drink?" I asked, walking over to my bar.

"Do you have any scotch hiding over there?"

"I do." I smiled and grabbed two glasses and a bottle of scotch. "Have a seat on my new couch, and let me know what you think."

"Damn, Miles. This is nice."

I handed him his drink and sat in the chair facing the couch.

"Are you officially a single man again?" Levi asked.

"I am." I tipped the glass to my lips.

"You could have stopped it. Honestly, I'm surprised you didn't."

"I have my reasons for going through with it. I need to show you something." I stood up, walked over to my desk, picked up the sonogram picture, and handed it to Levi.

"Is this—" He looked at me.

"Yes."

"Wow, Miles. How did you get this?"

"I went with Stella to her doctor's appointment after court."

Levi's brows furrowed. "She let you?"

"You sound like Isla. I didn't really give Stella much of a choice. She wasn't happy about it and told the doctor I was the sperm donor."

"Ha." He laughed. "So now what?"

"I don't know." I sighed. "I miss her, man. Three months ago, I was happy to go home and be alone. I craved it after a long day at the office. And now, it's the last place I want to go to at the end of the day."

"Look at you, Miles Bradshaw. You're growing up." Levi smirked.

"Shut the fuck up." A smile crossed my lips.

"Win her back," Levi said.

"She's so angry, Levi." I shook my head. "She hates me."

"She doesn't hate you. She's deeply hurt. You rejected her and your baby. Imagine how you would feel if someone did that to you."

I arched my brow at him.

"Your parents were a different situation. Put yourself in her shoes and go make things right. You're starting over, Miles. At thirty-two years old, this monstrous company is all yours. You love Stella, and you have a baby on the way. Life doesn't get any better than that, man." He smiled, standing up from the couch. "Thanks for the drink. I have to get going. Love the new office." He hugged me. "I'll talk to you later."

As I was sitting behind my desk, thinking about Stella, Isla walked in and set the bag with my sandwich in it on my desk.

"I also got you a grumpy-sunshine smoothie." She grinned.

"What the hell is that?" My brows furrowed.

"The deli you love so much now sells smoothies."

"Since when? I was just in there last week," I said, taking my sandwich out of the bag.

"They started selling them yesterday. They have a whole line with great names. They named that one after you."

"They did not." I narrowed my eyes at her.

"Yes, they did. I asked Owen, and he confirmed it. Taste it." She unwrapped the straw and stuck it through the lid. "Go on."

Shaking my head, I brought the straw to my lips and took a sip.

"Damn. This is phenomenal."

"See. Owen said you'll go from grumpy to a ray of sunshine after you drink it." A bright smile crossed her lips. "Anyway, where's your baby's picture? I bought this awesome frame that'll look great on your desk." She pulled the frame from the box.

I picked up the sonogram picture and handed it to her. She neatly tucked it into the frame and set it on my desk. I stared at it and smiled.

"I love it, Isla. Thank you."

"Excuse me? Say that again? I don't think I heard you correctly."

"I love it, Isla. Thank you. Now, get the hell out of here and get back to work."

She smirked, pointing her finger at me. "Ray of sunshine, boss. Ray of sunshine."

CHAPTER 27

Stella

I ordered room service because I didn't feel like leaving the hotel. I was tired and had a lot of homework to do since I missed my class this morning. I needed to find an apartment. It was ridiculous that in this large city, I couldn't find one that was suitable for my baby and me. This room was one of the bottom ones in the hotel—the cheapest and least favorite among guests. When the hotel asked if I planned on staying any longer, and I told them yes, they had to move me again because their other rooms were already reserved. Not this one. Nope. Nobody wanted to stay in this room.

I was eating my burger when I heard a knock at the door. I had called down earlier and requested more towels since the cleaning lady forgot to give me clean ones when she cleaned the room earlier. Climbing off the bed, I opened the door and froze when I saw Miles standing there.

"Hello, Stella."

"How did you know I was staying here?"

"May I please come in?" he asked.

"No, you may not."

He gripped my arms, lifted me up, moved me to the side, and stepped inside.

"Excuse me! What the hell, Miles?"

"I told you earlier we need to talk, and we're going to talk now."

"You didn't answer my question? How did you know I was staying here?"

"I had Sean follow you." He looked around the room. "Why this room, Stella? This is—"

"I know." I put my hand up. "This is all they had available."

"You lied to me," he said, sitting on the edge of the bed. "You said you were in an apartment."

"Why did you have Sean follow me? That was a shit thing to do, Miles."

"I was worried about you and your living arrangements. Why are you still in a hotel?"

I sighed and rolled my eyes. Climbing on the bed, I grabbed my plate and took a bite of my burger. Miles turned around and faced me.

"The entire time we were together, I never saw you eat a burger," he said.

"I don't really like burgers." I popped a fry in my mouth.

"Then why are you eating one?"

"I was craving it."

"Have you or have you not found an apartment yet?"

"No. I can't seem to find one."

"How is that possible in this city?"

"I guess I'm being overly picky," I said, biting into my burger. "Something doesn't seem right with every apartment I look at. I want certain things, and each apartment doesn't fit the criteria."

"Like what?" he asked.

"Space. I want a big room for the baby so I can decorate it with everything I want. I don't know." I picked up my napkin and wiped my mouth. "I want it to feel like home when I step inside, and none of them have."

He stood up, grabbed one of my suitcases from the corner, and set it on the bed.

"Excuse me? What the hell are you doing?"

He opened the dresser drawers and started tossing my things into the suitcase.

"I asked you what you were doing?" I climbed off the bed. "Stop that right now!" I walked over and tried to grab one of my shirts from his hand.

"You're moving back into the penthouse." His eyes stared into mine.

"The hell I am, Miles." I yanked my shirt from his hand.

"This is why I wanted to talk to you, Stella. You're moving back in with me. I want you there, in my penthouse, with me. I want you back home." He ran his hand through his hair and sat on the edge of the bed.

"Miles," I softly spoke.

"I want you and our baby home. I'm sorry for everything, Stella. There's so much I want to say, but I don't know how. Everyone is right about me. I don't know how to live a life outside Bradshaw Capital."

I knelt and placed my hands on his knees.

"I don't believe that. You're a good man, Miles."

He breathed out a laugh. "Yeah, a real good man. A man who asked a stranger to marry him because his mother screwed him over before she died."

"You need to let that go."

He placed his hand on mine and interlaced our fingers, softly stroking my skin with his thumb.

"I miss you, Stella. I felt something when you ran into me in that hallway in Vegas. I couldn't stop thinking about you. And when I saw you banging on that slot machine, I had to talk to you again. You actually scared me."

"Why?" My brows furrowed.

"Because I've never had feelings for anyone like I do for you. I'm just terrified at the thought of screwing my kid up like my parents screwed me up."

"I don't think you'll do that. You're not your parents, Miles. You need to realize that."

"I promise to change if you come back home. I need you, Stella. I need you and our child in my life. Levi asked me not too long ago if I loved you. I told him I didn't know what love was. But the more time passed and I wasn't with you, the more I realized that I truly love you. I don't blame you if you hate me."

"I don't hate you, Miles. I couldn't, even if I wanted to." I smiled.

He brought his hand up to my cheek and softly stroked it as our eyes stared into each other.

"I need your help, Stella. You have my permission to shrink me any time you find it necessary." A smirk crossed his lips. "Come home with me."

"Are you asking me, your ex-wife, to be your girlfriend?"

"Yeah. That's exactly what I'm asking."

"What about all the baby drama? The crying, sleepless nights, toys everywhere. When you get home from work, it won't be quiet like you're used to."

"None of that matters anymore. I welcome the baby drama." He took hold of my arms and stood me up, placing his hands on my belly. "We made this baby, and I'm all in."

Wrapping my arms around his neck, I brushed my lips against his.

"Let's go home." I smiled. "Who am I to turn down a handsome man and a luxurious penthouse?"

"You're the beautiful and smart woman that I fell in love with. That's exactly who you are, Stella Harper."

CHAPTER 28

Miles

I helped Stella pack her suitcases, and we left the hotel. Sean took her luggage and put them in the back of the escalade.

"Welcome back, Stella." He smiled.

"Thanks, Sean."

When we stepped off the elevator, I took her suitcases to my bedroom. Stella followed behind and threw herself on the bed.

"Ah, I've missed this bed." She grinned.

Climbing on top of her, I kissed her lips. "You're never leaving it." I smiled. "It's all yours."

Our kiss turned into amazing sex. Being inside her filled me with happiness, as did just being with her. I needed to make some changes in my life, and bringing her home was a start.

She lay in my arms as I held her tight, vowing never to let her go again. As her head lay on my chest, she started laughing.

"What's so funny?" I smiled.

She lifted her head and looked at me. "When we were in Vegas, there was a mishap with my birth control."

"How do you mean?"

"After we'd had sex for the first time without a condom, I went back to my room to take my pill, and they were gone. I'd left them in the bathroom on the counter. I started freaking out, so Jordyn called and got the lady who had cleaned our room. She told me there were no pills on the counter when she cleaned up. I accused her of lying, and Jordyn had to step in. She went to the CVS down the street and got me the morning-after pill."

"But you still got pregnant," I said.

"Well, that's the thing. I didn't get pregnant at that time. Since my pills mysteriously disappeared, I had to call Dr. Gregario the second we got back to New York. It was all messed up, and then when we had sex again, you didn't use a condom. We were so into the moment that I didn't even realize it. That's when I got pregnant." She bit down on her bottom lip, staring at me. "I'm sorry."

I brought my hand up and stroked her hair. "Don't ever apologize for getting pregnant with my child. I do believe it was meant to be."

"You believe in that stuff?" Her brow arched.

"I didn't before, but I do now." I smiled. "Can you come to my office tomorrow? I want to show you it. I had it repainted, put up new artwork, and bought all new furniture."

"I'd love to see it." She grinned.

"That office will be our child's one day."

"Only if he or she wants to be a part of the company," she said.

"I can't wait to find out the gender. We'll be able to find out at the next ultrasound, right?" I asked.

"I really don't want to find out. I want it to be a surprise when I give birth."

"As horrific as that sounds, we need to plan for the child with the right colors and furniture. That all depends on whether it's a boy or a girl. Don't you want to decorate in either blue or pink? Knowing beforehand will allow—"

She leaned over and placed her fingers on my lips.

"You're having anxiety over not knowing, aren't you?"

"Yes, Stella. I am. I admit it."

"Okay, Miles. We'll find out before the baby is born."

"Well, it's your decision too. I mean, if you really want it to be a surprise."

"You hate surprises, and I respect that. We're finding out what gender our baby is at the next ultrasound. Now, shut up." Her lips pressed against mine.

I rolled her on her back and hovered over her.

"I love you." I stared into her beautiful green eyes.

"I love you, too." She smiled as my mouth smashed into hers.

⁓

"Good morning, Isla." I grinned as I set a coffee from Starbucks on her desk.

Her brows furrowed. "You bought me a coffee?"

"I did." I strolled into my office.

"What's going on with you?" she asked, walking in.

"I'm a happy man. Stella, my girlfriend, is back home with me."

"You mean your ex-wife." She smirked.

"Knock it off." I pointed at her. "We're starting over. In fact, she's coming in today to see my new office. Call the florist and have a dozen, no, make it two dozen red roses sent to the penthouse. I want the card to say: I love you. Love forever, Miles."

Isla stood there, furrowing her brows.

"What?" I asked, picking up the picture of my baby and staring at it.

"You've never had me send flowers to anyone unless they died."

I shrugged. "No one has ever been worthy. In fact, I want you to set up weekly deliveries. Schedule them for Fridays. Different colors each time."

"Seriously?"

"Yes, seriously." I cocked my head. "I need you to reschedule my lunch meeting with Poppy Meyers."

"Why?"

"Because I'm having lunch with my girlfriend today."

"Ms. Meyers won't be happy you're rescheduling," she said.

"I don't care. Just do it."

I was reviewing some proposals when my office door opened. Looking up, I saw my beautiful girlfriend standing there.

"Look at this office." She smiled.

"Come here." I held out my arms.

She set her purse down, walked over, and sat on my lap.

"I missed you." I kissed her lips.

"I missed you too. Thank you for the beautiful roses. I love them."

"You're welcome." I smiled. "So, you like the office?"

"I love it." She stood up and walked around. "Great colors and furniture. Very CEO-like. I'm going to take a wild guess and say that your mother hated the color gray."

"How did you know?" I narrowed my eyes at her.

"Just a hunch." She smirked. "The baby and I are starving." She placed her hand on her belly.

"Well, let's go take care of that right now." I grabbed my phone and placed it in my pocket.

CHAPTER 29

Stella

"Are we finding out the gender today?" Dr. Gregario asked as he moved the wand over my belly.

"We sure are," Miles said. "Wow. I can't believe how much the baby has grown in a month." He gripped my hand.

"Oh, look at that. I have a perfect view. Tell me what you see," Dr. Gregario said.

I studied the monitor and looked at Miles, who sat there with a wide grin on his face.

"That's my boy," he said.

"You are correct, Miles. Congratulations, you two. You're having a boy."

Tears filled my eyes as Miles leaned over and kissed me.

"We're having a boy, babe." He softly stroked my forehead.

"A beautiful boy." I smiled, bringing my hand up to his face.

Miles took the whole day off, and we went shopping for furniture for the nursery. When we entered the baby store, Miles wrapped his arm around me.

"See, aren't you glad we found out it's a boy? Now, we can shop accordingly." He grinned.

"Yes, babe." I patted his chest. "I'm happy we found out."

I was looking at a certain crib, and when I looked over, I saw that Miles was gone. Walking around the store, I found him standing in front of a display of furniture in dark gray.

"I was looking for you," I said.

"Sorry, sweetheart. This bedroom set caught my eye. I have a vision."

"And what is your vision, Miles?"

"Light gray walls with this dark gray furniture—the crib, dresser, chest, rocker, and bookcases. What do you think?"

"I do love it." I turned the price tag over, and my eyes widened. "Wow. It's very, very expensive."

"Really, Stella?" Miles furrowed his brows. "Nothing is too expensive for my son. You know money is no object. And the same goes for you." He placed his finger under my chin and kissed my lips.

"In that case, can we hire an interior decorator to decorate the nursery? A.K.A. Adalyn Grant?"

"As long as we get this furniture, of course. I'm meeting with Harrison tomorrow, and I'll mention it to him."

"Thank you. I love you."

"I love you too, sweetheart." Miles smiled.

After a long day of shopping, I wanted to go home, take a bath, and relax.

"One more store." Miles glanced at his watch.

"I'm tired, Miles. I want to go home."

"We will, sweetheart. Right after this store." He opened the shop's door, and we stepped inside.

I was incredibly happy that he was excited about the baby, but he was taking his excitement to a whole new level.

"Can we pick up dinner on the way home?" I asked him.

"We'll have dinner at home. Dora said it's in the warming oven."

"Okay." I lay my head on his shoulder as we left the store.

I let out a sigh of relief when we finally made it home. Walking into the bedroom to strip out of my clothes, I saw a garment bag neatly placed on the bed.

"What's this?" I turned to Miles.

"I have no idea. Unzip it and see."

Grabbing hold of the zipper, I unzipped the bag and stared at the champagne-colored short, beaded, off-the-shoulder, flowy dress.

"This is beautiful." I removed it from the garment bag. "What did you do?" I smiled, looking at Miles.

"Try it on."

"What is this for?" I stripped out of my clothes and slipped into the dress. "Can you zip me up?"

"I'd be happy to." His fingers zipped the back of my dress as his lips caressed my neck. "It's a perfect fit for now." He winked, placing his hands on my belly from behind.

"Very funny. Did you pick this out?" I turned around in his arms.

"I did. I saw it and knew you would look stunning in it." His lips met mine.

"Thank you, but what's the occasion?"

"Come with me and find out."

He took hold of my hand and led me up the stairs to the rooftop. I gasped when I saw a round table draped in white linen with two matching chairs. A beautiful floral centerpiece made of red roses and white geraniums with a candle in the center graced the table. Red and pink rose petals were scattered over the rooftop, and soft music played in the background.

"What is all this?"

"Dinner." A smile crossed his lips. "I may have told you a lie."

"I'm already guessing you did." I smirked.

"I hired a chef to cook us a special dinner tonight."

"For?" My brow arched.

"To celebrate finding out the gender of our kid."

"Okay." I smiled as he pulled out the chair for me. "It's a little elaborate. Don't you think?"

"Nothing is too elaborate for you, Stella. Get used to it." A smirk crossed his lips.

We were served a wonderful dinner with a delicious dessert to top it off.

"Oh my gosh, I'm so full." I placed my hand on my belly.

"I hope not too full for a dance." Miles smiled as he pulled a small remote from his pocket, and the song You Are The Reason by Calum Scott started to play.

Miles took my hand and helped me from my chair.

"I picked this song because every word of it represents how much I love you."

"Oh, Miles." Tears filled my eyes. "I love you, too."

We danced and held each other close. I lay my head on his shoulder as contentment and peace flowed through me. Right when the song ended, Miles got down on one knee and pulled a small velvet box from his pocket. Placing my hand over my mouth, tears streamed in my eyes.

"Here we go again." He smiled. "Stella, I know my first proposal to you was not romantic, even if it was a proposal at all. I wasn't a very good husband the first time, but I hope you'll give me a second chance to show you that I can be the best husband and man you deserve. I love you so much, sweetheart. I want to give you the world, my love, and my life. I didn't want to go through with the annulment, but I had to because I knew I'd win you back and wanted us to start over. I know your first ring wasn't anything special, and I hope this one makes up for it." He flipped open the box. "Will you do the honor of marrying me and become Mrs. Miles Bradshaw for a second time?"

I gasped when I saw the four-carat, flawless cushion-cut diamond ring with a diamond-accented shank.

"Yes, Miles. I will marry you again."

With a smile, he removed the ring and placed it on my left hand, bringing it to his lips. He stood up and placed his hands on each side of my face, wiping the tears with his thumbs as they fell down my cheeks.

"I love you so much, Stella."

"I love you too." Our lips met passionately.

"By the way. We're not getting married in a courthouse this time. I want to make that very clear," he said, placing his forehead against mine.

I laughed as the tears continued to fall. "It wasn't that bad."

"Yes, it was. You're going to have the wedding of your dreams, sweetheart."

CHAPTER 30

Miles

"Are they all in there?" I asked Isla.

"They are, boss."

"And the food?"

"Everything is all set up. They're waiting on you."

"Thank you." I smiled as I stood and buttoned my suitcoat.

I walked down to the conference room and stepped through the double doors. Standing at the head of the table, I stared at each of them—my friends.

"Shaun Kind, Sebastian Bennett, Harrison Grant, Jack Sutton, Colin Black, Asher Remington, Grayson Rhodes, Drew Westbrook, Max Hamilton, Oliver Wyatt, and Liam Wyatt. Welcome to Bradshaw Capital." A wide grin crossed my face. "The board members are waiting upstairs. If you follow me, we can get this over with and then celebrate with food and alcohol."

"Let's do it." Shaun grinned.

We went upstairs to the boardroom. When I opened the door, all eleven members stared at us as we walked in.

"What is going on here, Miles?" Peter asked.

"I called this emergency board meeting to let you all know that," I cleared my throat, "your services on this board and at Bradshaw Capital are no longer needed."

"Excuse me? You can't do that," Dominic, one of the other members, said.

"It's obvious you didn't read the company's bylaws that my mother and father wrote when they started this company. A board member may be removed without cause. You all know that if you crossed either one of them, you were gone. To be honest, I'm surprised they even kept you on as long as they did. I own fifty-one percent controlling interest in this company, which gives me the right to remove all of you. Bradshaw Capital is going in a new direction, which requires fresh, new blood on the board. Hence, these fine gentlemen." I held out my hand. "They are the new shareholders of this company, and we have all voted to remove you. I want to thank you for your services and your dedication to Bradshaw Capital over the years." I smiled.

"You'll be hearing from my lawyer, Miles!" Peter's tone was harsh as he pointed at me.

"Now, now, Peter." Shaun wiggled his finger. "Don't forget with whom you're dealing with. Have you forgotten our history? Everything done here today is legal and ironclad. But if you want to waste your time, go ahead. Just go relax on the golf course with your wife or your thirty-something mistress if you choose."

"Fuck you, Kind." Peter shook his head. "What about your uncle?" he asked me.

"My uncle has been taken care of. He and my aunt are set for life."

"Your parents would be so disappointed in you, Miles."

"And you know what, Peter? I hope they are." I grinned.

"Ta-ta." I opened the door and gestured for each of the old board members to leave. "Now that it's settled, let's go eat and drink!"

~

Two Months Later

Stella

I'd finally received my master's and received my acceptance letter into the doctorate program. It was important to Miles that we married before our son was born. I was happy he felt that way because I felt it, too, but wasn't sure how we'd pull it off.

One Friday night, he booked us a room at the Plaza Hotel. He said that Saturday was our day of pampering and relaxing, and we'd return to the penthouse on Sunday. I couldn't wait to have him all to myself. That night, we were walking hand in hand, and he led me to the hotel's Grand Ballroom.

"Wow. This is gorgeous." I smiled.

"It's fit for a queen, which you are." Miles smiled, taking my hand and pulling me into him for a dance in the middle of the room.

"What are you doing?" I laughed.

He snapped his fingers, and soft music began to play.

"Dancing with my future wife. What do you think? Shall we share our first dance as husband and wife here?"

"Here?" My brows raised.

"Yes. Do you love it, Stella? Can you envision our reception here, filled with all of our friends?"

"Yes, of course. Who wouldn't want their wedding reception here?"

"Then your wish is my command, darling. We will celebrate our wedding here with all our friends on Saturday, September 7th."

"Excuse me?" I nervously laughed. "That's in less than two months."

"I know, but don't you worry. I've hired the best event planner in New York, and he's taking care of everything, with our input, of course."

"What about the wedding ceremony?" I asked.

"I've already booked that. We're getting married on the Tribeca Rooftop. Surprise!" He grinned. "You said you love surprises, so you can't be mad."

"How can I be mad at you? You over-organized planning, little freak." I smirk.

"I'm not sure if that was a compliment or not." His eyes narrowed.

"And you never will," I whispered in his ear.

∼

"You look incredible." Tears filled Jordyn's eyes.

"Thanks, friend." I hugged her.

"No, no, no!" Ralph ran over to us. "No smearing the makeup. So, all the girls will walk down the aisle first, and then you, my perfect little pregnant bride, will make your grand entrance on the rooftop."

"Okay." I smiled, for I had a different plan.

Jordyn handed me my bouquet, and we headed to the rooftop. It was a beautiful, warm September day without a cloud in the sky.

The music started to play, and the girls made their entrance. Ralph looked me over to ensure I looked perfect.

"I'll be right back," I said as I walked away.

"Excuse me? What are you doing, Stella?" he shouted. "Your future husband is waiting for you!"

I opened the side door and saw Miles standing there with Levi. He looked so handsome in his black tuxedo, his hands folded in front of him. He hated surprises, but this was one I couldn't help but give him. I quietly stepped through the door, walked over, and tapped him on the shoulder. He turned around, and when he saw me, he placed his hand over his mouth as tears filled his eyes.

"Surprise." I smiled as a tear fell down my cheek.

He wrapped his arms around me and pulled me into an embrace.

"This is not how we rehearsed it!" I heard Ralph whisper from behind.

"My God. You look so beautiful, sweetheart." He broke our embrace, and I reached up and wiped the tears that fell from his eyes.

"I love you." I smiled brightly.

"I love you more." He pulled me into him one last time before the minister stepped in and asked if we were ready to be married.

After our beautiful ceremony and many pictures later, Miles and I took a carriage ride through Central Park.

"I can't believe you did that. Did you see the look on Ralph's face?" Miles laughed.

"No, but I'm sure it was priceless." I grinned. "Oh!" I placed my hand on my belly. "Your son wants to join in on the excitement."

Miles placed his hand on my belly and held it there, feeling the little kicks from our baby.

"I can't wait to meet him, Stella."

"I can't either, Miles." Our lips met.

CHAPTER 31

Miles

Levi walked over and hooked his arm around me. "I can't believe you, Miles Bradshaw, got married twice, and I haven't been married once yet."

"Your day is coming up, my friend." I smiled.

"Laurel's pregnant."

"What? Congratulations." I hugged him.

"Thanks. Don't let on that you know. She wants to wait to tell everyone."

"Our kids will be best friends." I held up my glass to him.

"And if I have a girl, maybe they can get married." He tipped his glass to mine.

"I think we can arrange that." I grinned.

I stared across the room at my wife as she talked with her friends. She was the most beautiful bride I'd ever seen, and she was all mine. She caught me staring, and a breathtaking smile graced her face.

After we celebrated, we left the Plaza Hotel and headed straight to my company's plane, where we would fly to Italy for a two-week honeymoon. I was slowly learning to let go of my workaholic ways. Most nights, I was home by seven o'clock and turned my phone off on Sundays. I promised my beautiful wife I wouldn't take any work calls on our honeymoon. Plus, my staff knew better than to try to contact me. Whatever happened while I was gone would be dealt with when I returned. Stella would have my undivided attention—the attention she deserved.

We spent the past two weeks touring, resting, and relaxing in Rome, Venice, and on the Amalfi Coast. It was an incredible honeymoon and one I would never forget. Once we returned to our normal lives in New York, I would return to work, and in a month, Stella would start her doctorate program.

"Oh my God, I'm so tired," Stella stumbled into the kitchen. "How the hell are you standing there, looking so damn perfect and not jet-lagged?"

A smile fell upon my lips. "Good morning, sweetheart." I kissed her. "And good morning to you too, little one." I leaned over and kissed her growing belly.

"My goodness, Stella. I know it's only been two weeks since I saw you last, but you've really popped out," Dora said.

"I know. I have to go shopping. Now that it's getting cooler, maxi dresses won't cut it anymore."

"Sit down, and I'll make you some tea."

"I have to get to the office." I kissed the top of her head. "Forgive me if I'm a little later tonight."

"I know. It's your first day back after two weeks off, and you'll have a battlefield to navigate."

"See, Dora. This is why I love this woman." I grinned.

Walking to my office, I smiled and said good morning to Isla.

"Welcome back, you ray of sunshine, you." She grinned.

"Did you miss me?" I set my briefcase down.

"Would you fire me if I said no?"

"Yes." I arched my brow.

"Of course, I missed you, boss." She hugged me.

"Let's get down to business." I took a seat behind my desk. "What disasters do I have to clean up today?"

Two Weeks Later

Stella

As I was sitting at the table, eating lunch, and scrolling through my phone, an email with my first-semester classes, including an online class, came through. I stared at the email as an uneasiness settled inside me. Something had been on my mind a lot since receiving my acceptance letter to the doctorate program—conflict—undeniable conflict.

Later that evening, when I heard the elevator come up, I walked into the foyer to greet my handsome husband. The doors opened, and a smile fell upon both of our lips.

"You sure are a sight for sore eyes." Miles set his briefcase down and hugged me.

"I missed you." I broke our embrace and kissed his lips.

"I missed you too, babe. It's been a long day."

"Go sit down at the table, and I'll serve dinner. Dora made your favorite tonight."

"Chicken parm?" His brow arched.

"Yes. Chicken parm."

"I'll meet you in the kitchen after I change." He kissed my forehead.

While we sat at the table and had dinner, Miles told me all

about his day. I listened and asked questions to deter him from asking about mine. It worked, at least for a little bit.

"I'm going to take a bath." I smiled.

"That's a good idea. I'll join you." He grinned. "You start the bath water, and I'll clean this up." He grabbed the plates from the table.

I started the water, grabbed two towels, and hung them on the hook by the bathtub. As I twisted up my hair, Miles walked in, stripped out of his clothes, and climbed into the tub. I smiled as I stared at his hot ass through the mirror. Slipping out of my dress, I stepped in and leaned my back against his muscular chest as his arms wrapped around me.

"Pretty soon, my arms won't be able to do this," he said.

"You're an asshole." I laughed.

"That may be, but I'm your asshole." His lips pressed against my neck.

"There's something I need to tell you," I said, my fingers softly stroking his arm.

"Okay."

"I've decided to put my doctorate on hold."

"What? Stella, why? That's your dream."

"I know. It still is, and I will do it. I've been giving things a lot of thought, Miles. It's going to take at least four years and an internship. We have a baby on the way, and he's my priority."

"Oh, sweetheart. You can do both."

"I know I can. It's not about that. It's about not missing the milestones our child will reach because either I'm in classes or my nose is buried in a book. Getting my doctorate right now isn't as important to me as spending as much time as I can with our son."

"You know I'll be here to help you."

"I know." I tilted my head back and smiled. "I just don't

want any regrets when it comes to him. I won't regret putting off my doctorate. I'm still young and have plenty of time. But I will regret not being there for him. I've made up my mind, Miles, and don't think you can change it."

"First of all, I would never challenge you or your decisions. Second, I'd be the stupidest man on earth to even try." He breathed out a laugh. "I respect your decision, and when you're ready to go back and start that journey, I'll be right here cheering you on." His lips pressed against the top of my head as his grip around me tightened.

"Thank you, Miles. I was afraid you wouldn't understand."

"I understand perfectly, sweetheart. Now, I need you to understand that we need to get out of this tub so I can fuck you."

I threw my head back, laughing as I stared up at him.

"Is that all you think about?"

"Yes. And you're one to talk, missy. I still can't get the other day out of my head."

"What can I say? Pregnancy hormones." I grinned.

CHAPTER 32

TIME FLIES WHEN THE BABY IS COMING

Miles

I was in the middle of a meeting when the conference room door opened.

"Miles, Stella just called. She's been trying to get ahold of you. Her water broke, and she's on her way to the hospital."

"What? Now?"

"Yes, boss. Now."

I pulled my phone from my pocket, and it was dead.

"Shit. Sorry, gentlemen. We'll have to pick up this meeting another time. My wife is in labor." I smiled, running out of the conference room.

"I already called Sean. He'll be here in two minutes," Isla said.

"Thanks, Isla." I stepped into my office, grabbed my phone charger, and threw it in my briefcase. "Do me a favor and call the florist. I want five dozen white and blue roses arranged nicely in vases delivered to the hospital immediately. Stella will need visualization while she's in labor."

"And you know that how?" Isla said.

"I just do. Also, have a bouquet of balloons sent—all blue and some that say It's a Boy."

"On it. You better call me when the baby is born."

"I will." I smiled as I ran out of my office and headed down to the lobby. "Sean, I need to use your phone," I said, climbing into the front seat of the Escalade.

"Here you go."

I dialed Stella's number, and she answered on the first ring.

"This better be you, Miles!"

"It is, sweetheart. I'm on my way now. Sean said we'll be there in ten minutes."

"Is your phone dead?" she shouted. "Did you forget to charge it again, Miles?"

"Yes, sweetheart." I glanced at Sean.

"You're the CEO of a multi-billion-dollar company, and you can't even remember to charge your fucking phone!"

"Sit tight, babe. I'll be there shortly."

She hung up without saying a word.

"I think you're in the doghouse." Sean smirked.

"Good thing I told Isla to send five dozen roses and a bouquet of balloons to the hospital." I sighed.

Sean pulled up to the hospital's entrance, and I took the elevator to the labor and delivery unit.

"How can I help you?" a voice asked through the speaker.

"My wife is here in labor. Her name is Stella Bradshaw."

"Oh, hey, Mr. Bradshaw. She was talking all about you. I'll buzz you in."

When the door opened, a nurse was standing there.

"I feel like I already know you." She grinned. "I'm Pepper, Stella's nurse. My shift just started and I'm pulling a double, so I'll be with the two of you all day and night."

"You think it'll take that long?" I asked as she took me to Stella's room.

"Ha." She breathed out a laugh. "I love first-time dads."

When I stepped into the room, Stella lay on the bed, hooked up to the fetal monitor.

"Baby, I'm so sorry." I ran over and kissed her lips.

A smile graced her face as she grabbed my tie. "A dead phone? You forgot to charge it one week before our baby is due?"

"You're right. I'm an idiot, and I promise to make it up to you. How are you feeling? Are you in pain?"

"A little bit. It's not too bad yet."

"Good." I kissed her forehead. Unbuttoning my sleeves, I rolled them up. "All that matters is I'm here now, and we're doing this together."

~

Stella

The contractions started to peak with greater intensity. I moaned, laying on my side, gripping the bar of the bed, while Miles rubbed my lower back.

"Where is Dr. Gregario?" I asked Pepper.

"He's doing a C-section right now. He'll be in as soon as he's finished."

The contraction subsided, so I rolled on my back and looked at Miles. Bringing my hand up to his face, I softly stroked his cheek.

"Thank you."

"No need to thank me, sweetheart. I hate seeing you in so much pain. I'm going to get you through this."

"I love you."

"I love you more." He leaned over and kissed me.

"Happy Labor Day!" Dr. Gregario strolled into the room with a smile on his face. "How are you feeling, Stella?"

"How do you think?" My brow arched.

"Yep. Same response all my laboring mothers give me." He winked. "Let's see. Three hours ago, when you came in, you were dilated to three. I'm going to take a look and see if you've made any improvement." He lifted up the sheet and examined me. "Oh boy. You're still dilated at three centimeters."

"How is that possible?" I asked.

"It's common for first-time mothers. Don't stress about it. It'll happen. If you really want to get the ball rolling, I like to suggest to my patients that they try dance therapy."

"Huh?" My brows furrowed.

"Put on some music you like dancing to and start getting jiggy. Miles, just make sure you're close to her for when another contraction hits. As soon as it's over, start dancing again. I'll be back in a while." He left the room.

I looked at Miles, and we both furrowed our brows at each other.

"I'm seriously starting to think there's something wrong with that guy," Miles said.

"Me too."

"Ah, Dr. Gregario said to have you try dance therapy." Pepper smiled, walking into the room. "I know you might think it's weird, but it does work. I can see you're on the fence, so I'm going to dangle a carrot in front of you. Get to four centimeters, and a certain handsome anesthesiologist will come up here, give you an epidural, and all your pain will go away."

"Like, how fast does the epidural work?" I narrowed my eye.

"Within ten to twenty minutes," she said. "Pain-free, Stella. Imagine it." She waved both her hands in front of me.

"I'm in," I said.

"Awesome sauce. I'll unhook the fetal monitor."

After Pepper unhooked the fetal monitor, Miles took hold of my hands and helped me up from the bed. Another contraction hit.

"Oh, God," I moaned, leaning over the side of the bed.

"As soon as it passes, we'll dance," Pepper said.

"I've got you, sweetheart." Miles rubbed my shoulders from behind.

The contraction passed, and Pepper put on the song In Da Club by 50 Cent.

"This is one of my favorites." She smiled as she started dancing. "Come on, Stella. Just forget you're pregnant and move that body. Pretend we're at a club."

I started dancing to the beat of the music. It wasn't so bad.

"Come on, Daddy! Get down with us!" Pepper shouted.

"I'm good." Miles smiled.

"Now, Miles!" I shot him a look.

"Okay. Whatever you say, sweetheart." He began moving his body to the beat.

I made it through two rap songs before another contraction hit. I grabbed onto Miles as my body leaned against him. Pepper stopped and began massaging my back.

"It's okay. Breathe in and out," she said.

A woman knocked on the door and rolled in a silver cart filled with roses and a bouquet of balloons. Pepper turned off the music.

"Mrs. Stella Bradshaw?" the woman asked.

"Yes."

"We have quite a delivery for you." She smiled.

I glanced at Miles, and a smile crossed his lips. His eye winked at me.

"You did this?" I asked, climbing into bed.

"Of course. I'd be a little concerned if someone else sent you five dozen roses. They're for you to admire while trying to get through this labor."

"I love you, Miles."

"I know you do. I love you too."

"Let's check you out and see if anything is happening down there," Pepper said. "Woot! You're at four centimeters, Stella. I'll go let Dr. Gregario know, and I'll get that handsome anesthesiologist up here with those drugs."

CHAPTER 33

Miles

Ten minutes into the epidural, Stella was relaxed. The pained look on her face was gone, and the brightness returned to her beautiful eyes. She was so relaxed that she let me take a few work calls while she was on Facetime with Jordyn.

A few more hours had passed, and she was finally dilated to ten centimeters.

"It's time to start pushing, Stella." Dr. Gregario smiled.

She pushed for over an hour and was exhausted.

"I can't do this." Tears filled her eyes.

"Shh. That word isn't a part of who you are." I placed my hand on the back of her neck and leaned in so my face was touching hers and my lips were to her ear. "You got this, baby. Push."

She did as I asked, and I continued whispering in her ear.

"You are so strong. You're my beautiful wife, and I love you so much."

"Come on, Stella. That's it. One more big push," Dr. Gregario said.

"Do me a favor, baby. Give me everything you got. Our son is almost here, and he can't wait to meet his mommy. You got this, my strong girl. Come on," I whispered in her ear.

She pushed as hard as she could. Suddenly, my son's cries were heard. Tears filled my eyes as I kissed Stella's head. My bottom lip quivered as Dr. Gregario held our son up, and I cut the cord.

"He's beautiful, Stella."

The nurse took him, cleaned him up, weighed him, wrapped him in a blanket, and placed him in Stella's arms.

"Welcome to the world, Benjamin Miles Bradshaw." She softly kissed his head.

"Hey, buddy." I placed my hand on his head as tears streamed down my face. "God, Stella. He's so tiny."

"I wouldn't say that," Dr. Gregario said, stitching Stella up from her episiotomy. "An eight-pound baby isn't that tiny."

"If you say so, Dr. Gregario." I smiled as I stared at my son, softly stroking his head.

"You can hold him." Stella smiled.

"I want to, Stella, but I'm scared. He's so tiny."

"As I said—"

"Be quiet, Dr. Gregario," Both Stella and I spoke at the same time.

"Come on, big guy." Pepper patted my back. "Go sit in the rocker, and I'll show you how to hold your baby."

I sat down in the rocker, and Pepper placed Benjamin in my arms.

"Just make sure to support his head. Once this little guy has that down pat himself, you can toss him up in the air." She winked.

I sat there, slowly rocking, as I held my newborn son in

my arms. Tears streamed down my face when the thought that I wanted nothing to do with him when Stella told me she was pregnant came to mind.

"I will never fail you, my son. You have my word." I raised my arms and brought him to my lips.

∼

Two Weeks Later

"I don't give a rat's ass in hell what you have to do, Bob. Get that fucking deal closed!" I shouted as I paced around the living room.

"Shh! You're going to wake up the baby," Stella whispered.

"Sorry." I mouthed to her.

"Bob?" I spoke quietly and calmly. "Do you like your job? Then do it and do it right. I'll be back in the office tomorrow." I ended the call.

"Why don't you two lay down and nap?" Dora said. "I'll keep an eye on the baby. You two look exhausted."

"I think we'll take you up on that offer, Dora." I grinned. Walking over to Stella, I helped her up from the couch. "Come on, sweetheart."

"Thanks, Dora." Stella smiled.

We went into the bedroom and shut the door. Climbing on the bed, I rolled on my side and faced my beautiful wife.

"Who knew having a baby would be this exhausting," I said.

"I did." She smirked.

"But he's worth every sleepless night, every cry, and every diaper he explodes through." I smiled.

"I'm going to be sad when you go back to the office tomorrow. I kind of like having you around." She placed her hand on my chest. "Are you going to cry when you have to leave him?"

"Baby, I cry every day when I have to leave you."

"Shut up." She smacked me.

We managed to get a couple of hours of sleep. When we woke, we went to the living room to check on Ben, who was still sound asleep in his swing.

"Feeling refreshed?" Dora asked.

"We are, Dora. Thank you."

"Did he ever wake up?" Stella asked.

"Nope. That little angel has stayed sound asleep."

"Of course," I sighed. "This means he'll be up all night."

"He'd be up all night, regardless, Miles. Welcome to parenthood." Stella smirked.

"A flower delivery came for you while you were asleep. I put it in the kitchen."

Stella and I walked over to the island. "I wonder who this is from?" Stella asked.

"Let's find out." I removed the card while Stella unwrapped the large arrangement. "It's from Nadine and Brandon Kensington."

"Wow. This is beautiful. By the way." Stella looked at me. "I completely forgot to ask you something. Before we got back together, I ran into Nadine at a deli. She apologized and said she told her social circle that she lied about me stealing from them and trying to sleep with her husband. Did you have anything to do with that? Because Nadine wouldn't do that from the bottom of her heart. She's as cold as they come."

"I may have told them to set the record straight where you were concerned."

"And they just listened to the almighty Miles Bradshaw?"

"They did when I threatened to spill the tea to their circle about their financial woes." A smirk crossed my lips.

"Seriously?" Stella's eyes widened. "Financial woes?"

"Yep. Big ones." I wrapped my arms around her and pulled her into me. "Now, let's go wake our son up and play with him."

"If we wake him up, he's going to want to eat," she said, running her fingers through my hair.

"Better yet." A smile crossed my lips. "There's nothing more beautiful than watching you breastfeed our son." I leaned in and kissed her.

~

A heaviness settled in my chest as I stood before the headstones of my mother and father. Kneeling, I set a bouquet of flowers on my father's grave, then my mother's. This was the first time I'd been to the cemetery since her death.

"I hated you for what you did," I said as I stared at her name etched into the headstone. "But I'm happy you did it. I would never have met Stella and wouldn't have a beautiful baby boy. The scars of my past will always be there, but they will no longer define who I am. I will always be there for my son, no matter how busy I am. If he chooses to play sports, I will attend every single game, cheering him on. I will be there for him when he needs help with his homework. When he gets hurt, I'll be there to take away his pain. I'll make sure he feels the love I have for him, and I won't let a day go by where I don't tell my son that I love him. He will know what love is. Goodbye, Mom. Goodbye, Dad." I stood up, tucked my hands into my pants pockets, and headed to the car.

"Are you okay, Miles?" Sean asked, staring at me through the rearview mirror.

"I've never been better." I smiled.

CHAPTER 34

SIX MONTHS LATER

Stella

"Who is the most handsome boy in the world." I smiled, holding Ben up in the air.

"I thought I was," Miles said, pulling one of his ties from the closet.

"You're the sexiest man in the world." I smiled, and suddenly, a wave of nausea hit me.

I sat down on the edge of the bed, holding Ben on my lap.

"Sweetheart, are you okay?"

"Yeah, I'm fine." I waited for the nausea to pass. "Can you take the baby for a minute?"

"Of course." He walked over and took Ben from me. "Are you sure you're okay?" His brows furrowed.

Placing my hand over my mouth, I jumped up from the bed and ran into the bathroom. Miles followed and stood in the doorway. When I was finished, I grabbed a tissue and wiped my mouth. Standing up, I turned and faced my husband, holding our six-month-old son.

"Stella, are you—"

I slowly shook my head. "No. I can't be. It's probably the

food we ate last night." I left the bathroom and sat on the edge of the bed.

"We both ate the same thing."

"Why do you assume I'm pregnant because I threw up?"

He glanced at his watch. "It's about that time." A smirk crossed his lips. "Let's see. If my calculations are correct, our children would be fourteen months apart."

"You—you stop it right now." I pointed at him as I stood from the bed and walked out of the room, hearing him chuckle.

Walking into the kitchen, I said good morning to Dora and made a cup of coffee.

"I hope that's decaf," Miles said, handing Ben over to Dora.

"What's going on?" Dora asked.

"Stella is pregnant." Miles smiled.

"I am not! Stop saying that." I leaned against the counter, trying to sip my coffee as waves of nausea overtook me. Setting my cup down, I ran to the bathroom off the kitchen. Shit. Shit. Shit. When I finished, I walked into the kitchen, where Dora and Miles stood staring at me.

"I'll make you some tea." She smiled.

"And I have to get to the office." Miles walked over and wrapped his arms around me. "I love you," he whispered in my ear and then kissed my forehead.

"I love you too." I placed my hand over my mouth and ran back into the bathroom. I heard Miles chuckle as he said goodbye to Dora and Ben.

After showering and getting dressed, I took my son with me to the drugstore, picked up a pregnancy test, and headed to Bradshaw Capital.

"Ah, my baby is here!" Isla jumped up from her chair and

ran over to us. "Hi, Stella." She smiled. "And hello, you handsome little man." She took Ben from his stroller.

"Hi, Isla. Is my husband in there?"

"He's in a meeting in the conference room."

"Okay. I'll wait for him."

"Would you mind if I kept him out here with me?" she asked.

"Not at all." I smiled.

I walked into Miles' office and into his private bathroom. Pulling the box from my purse, I took out the test, took a deep breath, and let the urine stream soak the test strip. Setting it on the counter, a rush of emotions flooded me like a turbulent storm swirling around in my chest. Gripping the edge of the counter, my gaze turned to the strip test as I watched the word *Pregnant* slowly appear in the faintest pink and then darken as the seconds passed, confirming what I already knew.

"Stella?" I heard my husband's voice from the other side of the bathroom door.

Grabbing the stick, I held it behind my back. Opening the door, I stood there, staring at him as he held our son.

"Surprise." I held the stick up.

A wide smile graced his face as he set Ben on the floor and wrapped his arms around me, pulling me into a tight embrace.

"We're having another baby," he spoke with happiness.

"I guess we are."

"Are you not happy about it?" He broke our embrace.

"I am happy, Miles. Who wouldn't want two children under the age of two? I think we need to start interviewing nannies." I bent down and picked up Ben.

"Really? You said you didn't want one?"

"That was then. This is now." I smiled. "We're going to

need the help. Dora can't help with two kids and keep up with the house."

"Whatever you want, sweetheart." He kissed me.

Miles

I was happy—happy we were having a second child. Leaning back in my chair, I pulled my phone from my pocket.

"Grant Roman."

"Grant, it's Miles Bradshaw."

"Miles, it's good to hear from you. What can I do for you?"

"I'm in the market for a townhome."

"Excellent. I have a few listings. I'll email them to you now. Take a look and let me know what you think."

"Thank you, Grant. I'll be in touch."

After setting down my phone, I turned to my computer and opened my email, waiting for Grant's listings.

"Here's the proposal you wanted typed up," Isla said as she stepped into my office. "I could just eat up that baby of yours. He's so adorable. Why are you just staring at your computer like that?"

"I'm waiting for Grant Roman to send me some listings."

"Listings?"

"Stella is pregnant again."

"What? Oh my God, Miles. That's wonderful."

"Yeah." I smiled. "I'm not so sure she's thrilled about having two children under the age of two. I think it's time to move out of the penthouse and into a bigger home."

"Good idea. I'm heading to lunch. Can I get you anything?"

"No. I'm good. Thanks, Isla." I smiled.

The email I'd been waiting for popped up. Opening the listings, I carefully studied them.

Later that afternoon, my office door opened.

"Grant Roman is here to see you, boss."

"Oh? Send him in." I stood from my chair. "Grant." I smiled, walking over and extending my hand.

"Good to see you, Miles." He placed his hand in mine.

"Have a seat. What brings you by?"

"I was in the area showing an apartment and wanted to stop by and bring you this." He handed me a file folder. "It's not on the market yet, but it will be soon. The owner just filed for bankruptcy, and he needs to sell quickly. I wanted you to be the first to take a look at it. It's a hell of a deal for the Upper East Side."

I studied the listing and looked at the sale price.

"Seriously?" My brow arched.

"Seriously." Grant smirked. "We just got the call after I got off the phone with you."

"Set an appointment for tomorrow, and Stella and I will come look at it."

"Perfect. I'll get in touch with the homeowner and let you know a time."

I left the office around five o'clock. When I stepped out of the elevator, I heard Ben screaming as Stella walked around the living room with him, trying to console him.

"What's wrong with him?" I asked, setting down my briefcase.

"I think this little guy is teething. I gave him some Tylenol. Just waiting for it to kick in."

I took him from her, and he quieted down, laying his head on my shoulder.

"It's okay, Ben. Daddy's home." I kissed his head.

"Since Daddy is home, Mommy is going to take a long hot bath." She kissed my lips and walked away.

I took him into the nursery and sat in the rocker, rocking him and softly stroking his back. He fell asleep, so I carefully lay him in his crib. I walked into the bathroom and sat on the edge of the tub.

"He's sleeping?" Stella asked.

"Yes. I need to talk to you about something when you get out of the tub."

"It sounds serious? And frankly, I can't do serious right now, Miles. I need five."

"Five?"

"Five minutes to myself."

"Well, I think you've already had five minutes to yourself while I was getting our son to sleep."

"Have you already forgotten that I'm pregnant with your second child, and my hormones are all over the place?"

"Right." I leaned over and kissed her. "Relax, it's not that serious. We're moving." I walked out of the bathroom.

"What? Wait!" she shouted. "Miles, get back here."

I smiled as I changed out of my suit.

"What do you mean we're moving?" Stella walked into the bedroom, tying her robe.

"We're having baby number two. We need a bigger space."

"And this monstrous penthouse isn't big enough for the four of us?"

"It could be, I guess. But I want a townhome for us."

"Oh." Her eyes lit up.

"I knew you'd like the idea." I kissed her forehead. "Grant Roman sent over some listings earlier. He also brought me one in person. We're going to look at it tomorrow. It's in foreclosure, and the seller needs to sell it immediately. It's a hell of a deal." I walked out of the bedroom and into the living room, where my briefcase was. Opening it, I pulled out the listing and handed it to Stella. She took it and sat on the couch.

"Nine thousand square feet?" She looked at me. "Dora isn't going to like that."

"We'll hire her some help." I smirked.

"Oh, it has an exercise studio in the cellar. I think I like this already." She grinned.

My phone pinged with a text message from Grant.

"The homeowner will be out all day tomorrow. Will eleven o'clock work for you?"

"Eleven o'clock is fine. Thanks, Roman."

"Roman said eleven o'clock tomorrow morning to tour the home. I'll have Sean pick you and Ben up." I smiled.

CHAPTER 35

Stella

When Sean pulled up to the curb of the home, Miles opened the door and helped me from the Escalade.

"Stella, this is Grant Roman. Grant, my beautiful wife, Stella."

"It's nice to meet you, Grant." I smiled, placing the pack of crackers in my left hand and extending my right.

"The pleasure is all mine, Stella." He shook my hand.

Sean took Ben from his car seat and handed him to Miles. As we walked up the steps to the beautifully white-bricked home, Grant opened the door, and we stepped inside.

"Wow." I looked around, feeling a welcoming vibe.

"This home features six bedrooms and six baths." Grant smiled.

We toured the six-story home as I ate my pack of crackers.

"Well, sweetheart?" Miles glanced at me. "What do you think?"

"It feels like home already, but—"

"But what?" His brows furrowed.

"There are some changes that need to be made."

"I agree. The whole place needs to be repainted."

"It does, but the kitchen needs to be remodeled," I said.

"Why? What's wrong with the kitchen?" he asked.

"I don't like the cabinets or the countertop. Dora won't either. Also, this half-wall needs to go, and the island needs to be extended. I can envision it now." I smiled, biting into another cracker.

"Do you know how much it'll cost to remodel this kitchen?" Miles asked.

Taking my son from his arms, I stared at my sexy husband.

"I thought nothing in this world was too expensive for our son or me." My brow arched.

Grant chuckled.

"I love it, Miles. The kitchen, not so much. We can hire Adalyn to help design it."

"Happy wife, happy life, Miles." Grant smirked.

"Okay. We'll make an offer and remodel the kitchen."

"Thank you." I grinned, kissing his lips.

Three Months Later

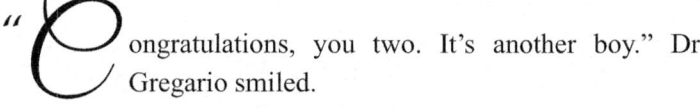

"Congratulations, you two. It's another boy." Dr. Gregario smiled.

"Ah, another boy." Miles leaned over and kissed my lips.

I was happy. As nice as it would have been to have a daughter, the thought of having two sons so close in age excited me. They would be brothers and as close as two brothers should be.

Miles helped me from the table and handed me my purse.

"Before I head to the office, let's go take a look at how the kitchen remodel is going." He hooked his arm around me.

We stepped into our soon-to-be new home. Painters were on each floor, painting the walls in the color we chose, gray. Bright white moldings and casings would grace the light gray walls throughout the house. Once the painters started and Miles looked around, he decided all the doors throughout the home needed to be replaced with six-panel doors painted white. I silently smiled because it was exactly what I thought.

"Wow. Oh wow!" I said, walking into the kitchen and looking at the brand-new Italian white custom cabinets that had been installed. My eyes diverted to the pristine white Italian marbled countertops with veins of gray throughout and the same marbled waterfall-styled island that stretched across the kitchen in all its natural beauty.

"This really makes the kitchen a lot bigger," Miles spoke.

"Do you love it?" I asked, running my hand along the marble.

"I do love it. Great idea, sweetheart." He winked.

"Mr. and Mrs. Bradshaw." One of the contractors walked into the kitchen. "All we have to do is hang a couple of more fixtures, and the kitchen is complete."

"Excellent. The painters are almost finished, and we'll be able to move in soon." Miles grinned. "I better get the moving company lined up."

I walked up the stairs and into the room that would be Ben's. We had it painted exactly how it was at the penthouse. Walking through the Jack and Jill bathroom, I stepped into the other room, which would be turned into a nursery. Miles walked in and wrapped his arms around me from behind.

"What do you want to do with this room? Now that we know it's a boy, we need to pick a color and tell the painter," he said.

"Pewter blue." I opened my purse, took out the paint sample, and held it up against the wall.

"Wait a second. "When did you get that sample?" Miles asked.

"When we went and picked the color for the rest of the house."

"Did you also pick any pink colors?" His brow arched.

"Nope. Just this one. I knew it was a boy. I could feel it." I smiled.

~

One Month Later

Miles

"Be careful with that piano!" I nervously spoke.

"Miles, they're professionals. They know what they're doing." Stella smirked.

"Oh my God. This kitchen!" Dora held out her arms.

"Right?" Stella grinned.

I smiled as I shook my head and went to make sure the movers were properly placing the furniture. We were fully moved out of the penthouse, and it was officially up for sale. Grant told me he had a prospective buyer already, and nothing pleased me more.

As I walked around our new home, I never saw myself in anything but a high-rise penthouse. Stella changed that for me. She changed a lot of things. She changed my entire life. I was the husband I never saw myself being and the father I never thought I'd be.

"All moved in?" I heard Levi's voice.

Turning around, he stood there with his hands tucked into his pants pockets.

"We're getting there, my friend." I walked over and hugged him. "What are you doing here? Shouldn't you be at the office?"

"I could be asking you the same thing." He smiled. "I was in the neighborhood and thought I'd drop in to see how everything is going. Wow. You and Stella did really good with this place."

"Thanks. We're going to be very happy here."

"I think Laurel and I will be too." A smirk crossed his lips.

"What do you mean?" My brows furrowed.

"The real reason I dropped by was to say 'howdy, neighbor.' I just closed on the townhome three down from you."

"Are you serious? I didn't know you and Laurel were looking."

"I wanted it to be a surprise. I told Grant not to say anything to you about it. After all, my Allie and your Ben are best friends and potential future husband and wife." He smiled.

"Congratulations, Levi." I hugged him. "I can't believe we're neighbors. Man, we're going to have some good times here." I placed my hand on his shoulder. "Stella!" I shouted. "Come in here."

"Did you tell him?" Stella asked Levi with a smile.

"You knew?" I cocked my head.

"Of course, I knew. Laurel is one of my best friends."

"And you couldn't tell me, why?"

"Because I know how much you love surprises, babe." She patted my chest.

"You wait until later." I pointed.

"If that's a threat, I'm looking forward to it." A sly smile crossed her lips.

CHAPTER 36

FOUR MONTHS LATER

Stella

I stepped out of the shower, dried myself off, and stared at my oversized belly in the mirror. I was due next week and couldn't wait to get this child out of me. As I walked into the bedroom, I stopped when I felt something trickling down my legs. Frowning, I mustn't have dried off good enough. Walking back into the bathroom, I grabbed the towel, and suddenly a gush hit the floor.

Grabbing my phone from the nightstand, I called Miles.

"Stella, are you okay?" Dora answered.

"Dora? Why are you answering his phone?"

"He left it on the table when he went to work. I was going to tell you when you came down, but you haven't been down yet."

"My water broke. Can you call Sean and have him get here to drive me to the hospital?"

"Of course. I'll call him now. Do you want me to call Miles at the office?"

"No. I'll take care of that. I'll be down as soon as I get dressed."

Sitting on the edge of the bed, I dialed his office number.

"Mr. Bradshaw's office. This is Isla."

"Isla, it's Stella."

"Hi, Stella. How are you?"

"Mr. Bradshaw left his phone at home, and I'm not sure how he hasn't realized it yet. Is he there?"

"He's in an important meeting in the conference room."

"Well, you can tell him that my water broke, and I'm heading to the hospital. Tell him not to hurry since HE'S AN IDIOT WHO FORGETS HIS PHONE WHEN HIS WIFE IS DUE TO GIVE BIRTH IN ONE WEEK!" I shouted.

"Noted," she said. "Yay! Baby Bradshaw is coming. I'll tell Miles."

"Thank you, Isla."

I threw on some clothes, ran down to the kitchen, and picked Ben up from his booster chair.

"Mommy loves you so much." I hugged him tight and planted tiny kisses all over his face.

"Good luck, Stella." Our nanny, Melissa, smiled. "Don't worry about Ben. He'll be well taken care of while you're in the hospital."

"Thank you, Melissa. You are truly a Godsend."

"Stella, are you ready?" Sean walked into the kitchen.

"I am, Sean."

"Good luck." Dora hugged me. "I can't wait to see our new baby."

Miles

I was in the middle of negotiating a deal when the conference room door opened.

"Boss, your wife just called. Her water broke, and she's headed to the hospital."

"What?" I reached into the top pocket of my suit coat and pulled out Ben's play phone.

"Oh my God." I placed my hand on my head.

"Apparently, you left your real phone at home. Stella told me to tell you not to hurry over since you're an idiot for forgetting your phone when your wife is due to give birth in a week. She was very loud about it."

"Ah, shit. I'm sorry, gentlemen. We're going to have to reschedule this meeting."

"We understand, Miles." Gordon smiled. "Good luck with the baby and your wife." A smirk crossed his lips.

"Thanks. I'm going to need all the luck I can get." I walked out of the conference room. "Call the florist and have five, no, make it six dozen roses sent with a bouquet of balloons. Also, I need you to go to Tiffany's and pick up the necklace they have reserved for me. I was saving it for our anniversary, but I feel like I need to give it to her now—maybe after she has the epidural. Yeah. That would be a good time to give it to her." I ran to the elevator and pushed the button.

"Anything else?" Isla asked.

"That should do it. I'm sure she's bringing my phone with her, so text me when you arrive at the hospital with the necklace."

"Will do, boss. Good luck," she said as I stepped into the elevator.

I grabbed a cab to the hospital. When I reached Stella's room, she glared at me.

"I'm so sorry, sweetheart." I walked over and kissed her forehead. I pulled Ben's play phone from my pocket and held it up. A small smile forced its way to her lips.

"Your phone is right there," she said.

"You're here." Pepper smiled, walking into the room.

"Pepper, you're our nurse again?"

"I am. I was delighted when I saw transport wheel your wife up. Are we ready for baby number two?"

"As ready as we can be."

Stella's contractions were intense, and so was her grip on my hand.

"Oh my God. I need that epidural," she shouted.

"Dr. Gregario is on his way. He told me to see how dilated you are," Pepper said. She examined Stella and smiled. "You're at four centimeters. I'll call the anesthesiologist right now." She walked out of the room.

Shortly after, a woman walked in, pushing a cart of the flowers I ordered.

"Mrs. Stella Bradshaw, these are for you." She placed the vases of roses around the room.

"They're beautiful, Miles. Thank you. Holy shit!" she screamed. "After this baby is born, you're getting a vasectomy."

"Excuse me?" I cocked my head as I massaged her back.

"You heard me!" she shouted.

My phone dinged. Glancing at it, Isla's name appeared. Once Stella's contraction was over, I opened the text message.

"I'm here with the necklace."

"Take a seat in the lobby. She'll be getting the epidural soon."

"Will do, boss. You do realize I have work to do, right?"

"I know that, Isla, but I can't leave her right now. I'm already in the doghouse, and she told me I'm getting a vasectomy."

She sent ten laughing emojis.

I sighed in relief when the anesthesiologist walked in and administered the epidural.

"You're all set, Mrs. Bradshaw. You should be feeling some relief in ten to twenty minutes."

Fifteen minutes had passed, and a bright smile crossed Stella's lips.

"Feeling better, sweetheart?" I stroked her forehead.

"Much better."

"Would you mind if I ran to the cafeteria real quick?"

"No. Go ahead. I'm just going to play a game on my phone until Dr. Gregario gets here."

I ran down to the lobby and found Isla. I took the box with the necklace in it out of the bag and slipped it into my pocket.

"Thank you. I owe you for this."

"How about a raise?" Her brow arched.

"We'll discuss it after my son is born. Get back to the office and hold down the fort."

I walked back into Stella's room with a coffee in my hand.

"Is that all you got?" Her brows furrowed.

"Nothing looked good. I'll grab something for both of us after the baby is born. Now that you're relaxed, I have something for you."

"You do?" She grinned.

"I do." I took off my suit coat, pulled the box from the inside pocket, and handed it to her.

"Oh, Miles. It's beautiful." She examined the open heart diamond platinum pendant. What is this for?"

"It's for giving me two beautiful sons." I smiled.

"I love it. Thank you."

"You're welcome." I leaned down and kissed her lips. "You're still having the vasectomy."

"We'll talk about that later." My heart started racing.

Six hours later, our son, Brayden Michael Bradshaw, was born, weighing seven pounds and eight ounces.

CHAPTER 37

THREE MONTHS LATER

Stella

"Can I get you some more ice?" I asked Miles as he lay in bed.

"No. But you can give me my son." He smiled, holding out his arms.

I handed Brayden to him.

"How are you feeling?" I climbed on the bed next to him.

"Not too bad, considering my manhood got snipped."

"It was for the greater good." I smiled, kissing his lips. "You'll be okay, big guy."

"Where's Ben?"

"Downstairs with Melissa. She's playing with him. Are you emotionally okay?" I asked.

"What do you mean, sweetheart?"

"Knowing you can't produce any more children. Sometimes, for men, it can cause depression, stress, and even anxiety knowing what was done to them. After all, your manhood is a huge part of you, and I just want to make sure you're okay."

"I appreciate it, baby." He leaned over and kissed me.

"I'm fine with the fact that you forced me into making sure we never have more children." A smirk crossed his lips.

"You're an asshole."

"Language in front of the child," he said. "I'm kidding you, sweetheart. I'm good. And knowing that I don't have to worry every time I come in that beautiful pussy of yours is a good feeling. Ouch." He placed his hand over the fabric of his underwear. "I think I'll take that ice now."

"You need to stop thinking about sex." I smirked, climbing off the bed.

"You do know who you're talking to, right?"

"Yes." I leaned over, kissed his lips, and took the baby. "I'll be right back with your ice."

∼

Having two children under the age of two was exhausting, but we were grateful we found Melissa when we did. She was a nanny for six months for Jerome and Renae Rich. As far as I was concerned, they were worse than the Kensington's, and their three children were monsters.

I had put it out there in the nanny circle that I was thinking about hiring a nanny for us. When my nanny friend Yasmin called me and told me that Melissa was sobbing one day in the park, I knew I had to intervene. She was twenty-three years old and moved out of her parent's house in Long Island and moved to the city with her best friend. She dreamed of becoming a real estate agent, working for one of the many prestigious property companies in New York. She had experience with children, being the oldest of eight, and with parents who both worked. The Rich's hired her because they were desperate, and word in the nanny circle hadn't gotten to poor Melissa yet.

I visited the park one day with Ben. Melissa and I met and instantly clicked. I offered her more money than she was getting paid, and Miles was generous enough to pay for her health insurance. Now, I was known in the social circle as the nanny-stealing thief. Did I care? Not at all. I laughed about it, and so did Miles. I knew our time was limited with her because, one day, she'd get her real estate license and leave us for bigger and better things. That was okay, though. I wanted her to succeed and would help her in any way possible.

While my poor husband was in bed with an ice pack on his balls, I asked Melissa if she wanted to go shopping on Fifth Avenue. We got the children ready and climbed into the Escalade. I sat in the front, and Melissa sat in the back with the kids.

"Let me know when you're ready to go home." Sean smiled as he took the double stroller from the back and set it up.

"Thanks, Sean."

We went into Saks to look around. As we were shopping through the racks, Renae Rich walked over.

"Well, well. If it isn't Stella Bradshaw." Her eyes raked over me. "And you, Melissa." Her tone was snobby.

"Hello, Renae." I smiled. "Shopping for anything special?"

"Not really. Spending your husband's money?"

"Where are the children?" I asked and ignored her question.

"Please. I don't bring my children shopping. I have hired help for that. I don't need the aggravation while I'm trying to shop for myself. Stella, I don't want to bring this up, but nobody else in the circle has enough guts to."

"Okay?"

"You will never be accepted in our social circle. I mean, come on. You were a nanny, for goodness sake. I'm not quite sure why Miles Bradshaw chose you. Aren't you from Florida or something?"

"I am from Florida." I gracefully smiled even though I wanted to rip her face off.

"A Florida girl who sunk her claws into a billionaire and made sure she had children so she'd be set for life."

I looked at Melissa, who was standing there a nervous wreck, holding her phone.

"And then you go and steal our nanny right out from under us. You are nothing but a trashy Florida nanny-stealing thief who married a man to gain social status. We all know that you most likely fabricated a story that you were pregnant to get Miles to marry you the first time. But then he found out the truth and had your marriage annulled. Then you sucked him right back in when you found out you were pregnant with little Benjamin. That child probably isn't even his. You listen to me. We don't deal with trash like you. You are not a part of our circle, nor will you ever be."

That was it. My hormones were still flying high from the pregnancy, and I couldn't stand looking at her anymore. Taking my right fist, it accidentally hit her jaw and flew across her face. Melissa jumped and covered her mouth with her hand. The kids started to cry, and Renae Rich fell into a rack of clothes and onto the ground.

"How'd you like that, Renae?" I stood over her. "Florida trashy enough for you?"

"My nose. I think you broke my nose!" she screamed.

"Good. You needed a nose job to fix that botched job anyway."

Several sales associates ran toward us, and so did security.

"She did this! She did this!" Renae profusely yelled, pointing at me. "Call the police. I'm pressing charges against that psychopath."

"Mrs. Bradshaw, come with me." Charles, the security guard, took hold of my arm.

"Melissa, you have Sean's number. Call him right now and have him pick you and the kids up and go to the park," I shouted as Charles led me through the store. I turned my head. "And whatever you do, don't mention this to him. Make something up. I'll be fine."

He sat me in a room and kept an eye on me, so I didn't escape.

"What were you thinking, Mrs. Bradshaw?" He handed me an ice pack for my knuckles.

"Besides how badly I wanted to rip that gold-digging bitch's head off?" I cocked my head. "You know how they are, Charles. I'm not like them."

"I know." He shook his head. "She said she's pressing charges, so the police will be here soon."

"Great." I rolled my eyes. I wasn't surprised. Now, I gave the social circle more ammunition to hate me, not that I cared.

The door opened, and two police officers stepped in.

"Are you Mrs. Stella Bradshaw, ma'am?"

"Yes, I am." I stood up.

"Did you assault one Mrs. Renae Rich?"

"Yes, I did." I stood proud and tall. "If you're going to arrest me, please don't handcuff me and walk me out the back entrance. I will cooperate and go with you."

"Ma'am, we—"

"Please. I'm asking you nicely. I've already caused a scene here. Let's not cause another one." I bit down on my bottom lip.

"Fine. We'll go out the back entrance of the store. But if you try anything funny—"

"I won't. I promise."

The one police officer brought the car around to the back of the store, and I climbed into the backseat. Not only was I a nanny-stealing thief, but now I was a nanny-stealing thief felon. How could I lose control like that? What would Miles think of me now? The thought swirled in my head. This wasn't just about me. This was also about how it would reflect on him.

"Step behind the line," one of the officers spoke.

Great. They were taking my mugshot. I smiled as I held up the placard. Why not? Once they finished booking me, I asked for my one phone call. Dialing Miles's number, he answered.

"Miles Bradshaw."

"Hey, you. It's me. Your wife who loves you so much."

"Stella? Are you okay?"

"Well, no. I'm in jail, 24th precinct.

"JAIL!" he shouted. "Where are the kids?"

"They're with Melissa at the park."

"Ma'am, your time is up," the officer said.

I held up one finger to him.

"Miles, I'm being charged with assault."

CHAPTER 38

Miles

"Assault! Who did you assault?"

"Renae Rich. I'll tell you about it later. They're making me hang up. Help me, Miles!"

"Hello? Stella?" I shouted. "Fuck!" I jumped out of bed and grabbed my aching balls.

Scrolling through my phone, I dialed Elijah Wolfe.

"Elijah Wolfe," he answered.

"Elijah, it's Miles Bradshaw."

"Hey, Miles. How are you?"

"I wish I could tell you I was good, but my wife's been arrested."

"Arrested? For what?"

"Assault."

"Which precinct did they take her to?"

"The 24th precinct."

"I'm on my way."

"Thanks, Elijah. I'll meet you there."

I threw on a pair of sweatpants and a sweatshirt. I couldn't believe this. What on earth would possess my wife to assault Renae Rich? I hailed a cab to the 24th precinct.

"May I help you?"

"I'm Miles Bradshaw. My wife is being held here."

"Her name?"

"Stella Bradshaw."

"Her attorney is with her now. You may have a seat over there."

"Thank you."

I pulled out my phone and called Levi. Laurel answered his phone.

"Hey, Miles."

"Laurel, where's Levi?"

"He's in the shower. What's wrong?"

"Stella's been arrested."

"What? For what?"

"Apparently, she assaulted Renae Rich."

"It's about time somebody did. Good for her. I'll have Levi call you when he gets out."

"Okay. Thanks." I dialed Sean.

"Miles, what's up?"

"Where are you?"

"I'm waiting at the park for Melissa and the kids. Why?"

Get them and drive them home.

"What about Stella?"

"What do you mean? She's in jail, Sean."

"In jail! What are you talking about? Melissa told me that Stella decided to get her makeup done, and it was going to be a couple of hours and just to have me drive her and the kids to the park."

"Well, she lied. She assaulted Renae Rich."

"Ha." He chuckled.

"Sean, it's not funny."

"Actually, Miles, it is, and you know it. I see them. I'll take them home now and then come get you."

"Thanks. But I'm not leaving without my wife."

"Miles," Elijah said, walking toward me.

"Elijah, how is she?"

"She's okay. I was able to get an emergency bond hearing so we could get her the hell out of there. We need to be at the courthouse in an hour. In the meantime, I'll head back to my office and prepare."

"Did she really assault her?" I asked.

"Yes, and she proudly admits it. The officer said she broke Mrs. Rich's nose and bruised her eye. I guess she punched her right across the face." He smirked.

"Great. Just great." I sighed.

Sean picked me up, and we headed to the courthouse.

"Miles, I spoke with Melissa. She told me what happened."

"And?"

"Mrs. Rich started it by calling Stella Florida trash, and then she said she only married you for your money and fabricated some story about being pregnant the first time around. I think the word gold-digger was thrown in there. Then she said something about how Benjamin probably isn't even yours."

"That stupid bitch. This is all my fault."

"How?" Sean asked.

"Because nobody knows the real story about us. She's getting blamed for something I initiated and did."

"Miles, it's nobody's fault but Renae Rich's."

We walked into the courtroom and took a seat. When I turned around, I saw Stella and Elijah walk in.

"Sweetheart."

"I'm sorry, Miles." She twisted her face. "I love you."

"I love you too."

"Mr. Wolfe, how does your client plead?"

"Not guilty, your honor," Elijah said.

"Your honor," the Assistant District Attorney spoke. "There are several witnesses who saw Mrs. Bradshaw assault Mrs. Rich in the middle of Saks Fifth Avenue."

"Your honor, my client was provoked."

"Oh, come on, Elijah. It doesn't matter," the ADA said.

"Your honor, my client is an upstanding citizen, married to Miles Bradshaw, CEO of Bradshaw Capital. She has no priors and has never had a parking ticket. She has two small children at home, one of whom is three months old. She has a master's in child psychology and is pursuing her doctorate. A woman like her does not go around assaulting people unless they are provoked into doing so. Mrs. Rich publicly humiliated my client and harassed her as she was shopping with her nanny and two children. Therefore, we will be bringing a lawsuit against Mrs. Renae Rich for defamation of character and harassment."

"Bail is set at twenty-five hundred dollars cash. You will be notified with a trial date."

"Thank you, your honor."

The officers took Stella away and I looked at Elijah.

"As soon as you pay the bond, they'll process her release, and she can go home. I would suggest trying to get Mrs. Rich to drop the assault charges. If you need help, let me know. If she won't, we'll use any means necessary to tear that woman apart."

"Thanks, Elijah." I shook his hand.

I paid the bail and waited for Stella to be released. The moment the door opened and I saw her, I jumped up and hugged her.

"Are you okay?"

"I'm fine. I want to go home," she said.

"Let's go." I hooked my arm around her, and we left the building.

The moment we arrived home, Stella ran to the kids and hugged them.

"Melissa, I'm so sorry," she said.

"Don't be, Stella. You were the absolute best, and that bitch deserved it. You are truly my hero. I recorded her on my phone."

"You did?" I asked.

"Yeah. Just in case we needed it for something. But I stopped recording right before you punched her because I saw the look on your face when she said that Ben probably wasn't his child."

"Not my finest moment. Okay, it was. Who am I kidding?" Stella smiled.

I let out a sigh. "Sweetheart, I know she deserved it, but you were booked and thrown in jail."

"It wasn't that bad. I met a nice girl there. She was a prostitute but so sweet."

"Melissa, keep an eye on the kids while we go upstairs. Also, can you send me that recording?"

"Yeah. I'll send it now." She pulled out her phone.

"Come on, my little felon." I hooked my arm around Stella. "Let's go draw you a hot bath."

"And a glass of wine?" Her brow arched.

"And a glass of wine." I smiled.

~

Stella

"It's all my fault, Stella," Miles said as he sat on the edge of the tub and listened to the recording.

"How is this your fault? I'm the one who punched that bitch and broke her botched-up nose."

"Because nobody knows why we got married the first time. We're just letting everyone go around thinking that you trapped me with a fake pregnancy and I married you out of obligation."

"Since when does Miles Bradshaw care what other people think?" My brows furrowed.

"I don't. But when it comes to my wife, I do. Everything she spewed was a total lie."

"I know. She called me Florida trash. Can you believe that?"

"Well, I don't blame you one bit for punching her. I would have done a lot more damage than just a broken nose."

I started laughing.

"What's so funny?" Miles asked.

"You should have seen her lying there in the rack of clothes." I continued laughing. "And the look on her face. Shit, Miles. I'm in so much trouble. What are the kids going to say when they grow up and find out their mother is a felon?"

"Aw, sweetheart. They'll know you to be a strong independent woman who doesn't take shit from anyone. And you're not a felon. I will get Jerome to get that bitch wife of his to drop the charges."

"And how are you going to do that?"

He set his phone down and began rubbing my shoulders.

"The social elite women in New York have their secrets, and we rich men have our secrets amongst each other.

"Do you really think you can get him to get Renae to drop the charges?" I pouted.

"If he doesn't, Renae Rich will be sorry she ever spoke a word to you." He leaned over and kissed the top of my head.

"Oh my God, Miles. How are your balls? You were supposed to be resting all day."

"Sore, but I'll survive." He smiled.

I climbed out of the tub, and Miles wrapped a large soft towel around my body and pulled me into him.

"Miles?"

"Yes, sweetheart?"

"I want you to get in bed and relax. I'll get the ice packs and deal with the children." I broke our embrace.

"Stella, I'm—"

"Now, mister!" I pointed toward the bedroom. "Go."

I slipped on my robe while Miles climbed on the bed. Walking downstairs, Melissa played with Ben while Brayden sat peacefully in his swing.

"Thank you for staying, Melissa." I walked over and sat next to her.

"You don't have to thank me, Stella. I'm more than happy to stay and help with the children whenever you need me. You and Miles are like family to me."

"And you're like family to us, too." I smiled.

Melissa put Ben to bed for the night and went home. After grabbing an ice pack and Brayden, I went upstairs.

"Here's your ice pack, babe."

Climbing on the other side of the bed, Brayden latched onto my breast and began feeding.

"Did you ever think you'd be married to a criminal?" I glanced at Miles as he scrolled on his phone.

He chuckled. "You're not a criminal, sweetheart."

"Oh boy. I'm sure I'm the talk of Manhattan." I sighed.

"Let them talk. This is probably the most exciting gossip they've had in a long time." He winked.

CHAPTER 39

Miles

The next morning, I kissed my wife and kids goodbye and climbed into the Escalade.

"Morning, Sean."

"Morning, Miles. How's Stella?"

"She's fine. I need you to make a stop at the Rich's house before taking me to the office."

When I entered the building, the doorman called to announce that I was there. Jerome told him to send me up. Taking the elevator to the thirtieth floor, I stepped into the foyer.

"Miles." Jerome nodded, extending his hand.

"Jerome." I placed my hand in his.

"What is he doing here?" Renae walked into the foyer.

Her nose was covered in a white bandage, and the bruising below her eye was prominent.

"Renae." I nodded as I held back the laughter that wanted to escape.

"Are you here to apologize on behalf of your wife? Because if you—"

"I'm not here to apologize on behalf of my wife. I'm here to talk to Jerome."

Her one eye steadily narrowed at me.

"Let's go into my office." Jerome glanced at his watch. "I don't have much time, Miles. I have a meeting to get to."

"This won't take long," I said, following him to his office.

He shut the door and told me to have a seat.

"What is this visit about?" he asked, taking a seat behind his desk.

"I want you to get Renae to drop the charges against Stella."

"You know I can't do that, Miles. What Stella did was unacceptable. You really need to control your wife."

I could feel the rage brewing inside me.

Pulling out my phone, I played the recording for him.

"You're the one who needs to control your wife, Jerome."

He sighed and leaned back in his chair.

"You know how Renae is," he said.

"And you know how I am. I will go to any lengths to protect my wife and family."

"What do you want me to do?" He threw his arms out.

"You are to get Renae to drop the charges, or some information might get leaked about the mistress you're keeping in that apartment on the Upper West Side."

"You wouldn't dare."

"Wouldn't I?" My brow arched. "And what about the little mishap that occurred with one of your nannies a couple of years ago? The one you paid off to keep quiet after Renae physically struck her, and the poor girl fell, cutting her forehead and needing stitches? And let's not forget about the little drug problem your wife has. Norco's, isn't it?" I cocked my head. "The ones she illegally gets because her doctors won't prescribe them to her anymore."

"Enough, Miles."

"No!" I spoke through gritted teeth as I jammed my finger on his desk. "Renae deserved what Stella did to her, and you know it, Jerome. Your wife has a lot of issues, and she needs help. But instead of trying to help her, you avoid her. Just fucking divorce her, for God's sake."

"You know I can't do that."

"If Renae doesn't drop the assault charges, my attorney and I are prepared to file a lawsuit against her for defamation and harassment. She intentionally approached Stella in the middle of that store and harassed her. And once Elijah gets done with her, all of your dirty laundry will be aired."

"Elijah Wolfe?" he asked.

"Yes. Elijah Wolfe. He will destroy Renae, and you know it. If you think you have problems now, you haven't seen anything yet." I stood from my chair and buttoned my suitcoat. "You have twenty-four hours to get Renae to drop the charges. One minute past that, and we go to war, Jerome. Have a good day." I walked out of his office.

"If you're trying to get my husband to get me to drop the charges, you're crazy," Renae said, following me to the elevator.

"It's your funeral, Renae. You can either stop all this or suffer the consequences that are coming your way." I stepped onto the elevator. "Have a good day."

I climbed into the back of the Escalade and slammed the door.

"How did it go?" Sean asked.

"I think it went well. Now, we wait and see what happens."

Later that afternoon, I was sitting in my office when I heard a baby crying in the distance. I knew that cry, so I got up from my desk, opened my office door, and saw Stella walking toward my office, holding Brayden and pushing the stroller with Ben in it.

"Sweetheart." I smiled. "What are you doing here?" I took my son from her. "Where's Melissa?"

"I called her this morning and told her to take a couple of days off with pay. After yesterday, she deserves it."

Isla jumped up from her chair and took Ben from his stroller. Stella and I walked into my office. I held Brayden over my shoulder and softly rubbed his back.

"I have great news." Stella grinned. "Elijah called and said that Renae dropped the assault charges."

"That's wonderful, sweetheart." I smiled, kissing her lips.

"What did you do, Miles?"

"I told Jerome that all of their little secrets and dirty laundry would be aired for all of Manhattan to know if he didn't get Renae to drop the charges."

"Thank you. I love you so much."

"And I love you and our family." I wrapped my arm around her and pulled her into me. "It's over, my little felon." I kissed the top of her head.

"I still want to sue her, Miles."

"Let it go, Stella. Let it go."

CHAPTER 40

FOUR YEARS LATER

Miles

I loved my life. My company was stronger than ever. Stella had finally graduated with her doctorate, and our children were growing way too fast. Ben showed an interest in soccer, and for being six years old, he was a natural at it. I attended every practice and game. When I'd come home from work, I would sit down at the piano, both boys on each side, and play a song for them. My wife grew more beautiful each year, and I loved her even more, which I didn't think was possible.

"What do you think, Miles?" Grant asked as we walked around the space.

"I think it's perfect." I glanced at my watch. "Stella should be here any minute."

I stepped outside the building and waited for Sean to pull up. When he did, I opened the door and helped Stella and the kids out of the car.

"Daddy!" Brayden held up his arm, and I picked him up.

"What are we doing here?" Stella asked, looking at the building.

"Come inside, and I'll tell you." I smiled, taking hold of Ben's hand.

She said hello to Grant and looked around. "This is great, but I still don't understand why you brought me here."

"Come on, Brayden," Ben said as they both ran around, chasing each other.

"Say hello to your own practice, sweetheart." I grinned.

"What?" Her eyes widened. "Are you serious?"

"You're a Bradshaw, Stella. We don't work for anyone. People work for us." I smiled.

"Oh my God." She threw her arms around me. "I can't believe this. Thank you. Thank you." She planted tiny kisses all over my face.

The boys were wrestling on the ground, and Brayden was screaming.

"Boys, that's enough. Do you love this space, sweetheart?"

"I do." A beautiful grin crossed her lips.

"Then it's settled. "Grant, you just sold a building."

"Excellent. I'll call you as soon as the paperwork is ready." He shook my hand.

"I can't believe you did this for me?" Her arms wrapped around my neck.

"You know I'd do anything for you." I smiled as the kids ran around us, screaming. "Why don't you give Adalyn a call, tell her the good news, and talk design with her? Do anything you want to this place. I'll take the boys back to the office with me so you can have the rest of the day to yourself."

Sean drove us to my office.

"You boys be good for Daddy." Stella kissed them good-bye. "I love you." She smiled.

"I love you too. Enjoy the rest of your day." I kissed her.

I took the boys up to my office. They immediately ran to Isla, who was like an aunt to them.

"How did Stella like the building? she asked.

"She loved it." I grinned.

"Daddy?" Ben said. "Can I sit in your chair?"

"You sure can, buddy."

He ran over and sat in my chair, placing his hands on my desk.

"That right there is the future of Bradshaw Capital." I glanced at Isla.

"And what about that one?" she pointed to Brayden as he wildly jumped on the couch.

"I'm not sure about him yet. Brayden, we don't jump on the furniture." I sighed.

～

*S*tella

I had a space—not my office space, but a space in my home where I go when I need to destress. It was a quaint little corner with a comfy chair, a salt lamp, and an essential oil diffuser. It was a space where I studied and where I would go when the kids were out of control. When I would tell them Mommy needs five, they knew to leave me alone for a few moments. It was my sanctuary.

I had the perfect life: a loving husband, two beautiful sons, and I'd finally become Dr. Stella Bradshaw. The journey wasn't easy, but with the support of Miles and my friends, I'd made it. And now, I'd start my own practice and help families and their children in need.

～

Two Years Later

Miles

When I opened the front door, the boys were running around the house, chasing each other with their play swords.

"Hi, Dad." Ben smiled, running past me.

"Where's your Mom?" I asked.

"She said she needs five."

I smiled as I walked up the stairs and to her sanctuary. I stood in the doorway and stared at her as she sat there with her eyes closed.

"The boys said you needed five." I smirked.

Her eyes opened, and a smile graced her beautiful face.

"I actually need thirty."

I chuckled as I walked over and sat on the floor next to her.

"Tough day, sweetheart." I took hold of her hand.

"A little bit, but nothing I can't handle."

I leaned over and kissed her lips. "Take all the time you need. I'll take the boys to the park and let them get out all their energy."

"You're the best. I have patient notes to catch up on."

"You do that." I stood up. "I'll bring dinner home for us, and once the kids are in bed, we'll take a hot bubble bath, drink some alcohol, and then I'll have my way with you in bed."

"Sounds like a dream." She smiled.

I sighed when I heard Brayden crying.

"Dad, Brayden fell and hurt himself," Ben yelled.

"He pushed me!" I heard Brayden shout.

I looked at Stella and sighed. "When does our new nanny start?"

"Next week." She smiled.

EPILOGUE

Miles

As the years passed, both of our boys graduated high school with honors, attended Columbia University, and came to work for Bradshaw Capital. This was their legacy, and I couldn't have been prouder of them.

"Dad, I closed the deal with Hemingway," Ben said, walking into my office.

"Excellent, son. Don't forget family dinner is tonight."

"I know. Mom already called me this morning." He smiled. "Allie won't be able to make it. She has classes."

"How are things between the two of you?" I asked.

"Things are great. There's something I want to talk to you about."

"Okay."

"I'm going to propose to her on her birthday next week. We've been dating for years now, and I love her so much and want her to be my wife."

"That's wonderful, son." I stood up, walked over, and hugged him. "You already know we love her."

"I know. She loves you guys, too."

"Did you pick out a ring yet?"

"Yeah. I bought it a couple of days ago."

"Wow, I can't believe my son is getting married. Your mom is going to be over the moon. You better tell her tonight."

"I will." He chuckled.

I left the office and headed home. When I walked through the door, Stella wasn't home yet from work. After changing my clothes, I heard her calling for me. Running down the stairs, I took her in my arms and kissed her.

"Sorry, I'm late," she said. "I ran a little over with a patient."

"No worries, sweetheart."

"I stopped and picked up dinner for all of us. The boys should be here soon."

"I'll set the table," I said, reaching up into the cabinet and pulling down the plates.

We heard the front door open and the voices of our boys.

"Hey, parents." Brayden smiled.

"Hello, son." I hugged him. "Hi, Delilah." I hugged her.

Brayden and Ben kissed Stella's cheek, and we all went into the dining room for dinner. Something was off with Brayden. He seemed nervous. As we were eating, he said he had an announcement to make.

"Mom. Dad. Ben. I asked Delilah to marry me, and she said yes." He grinned.

Delilah placed her ring on her finger and held her hand out.

"Oh my God. That's wonderful." Stella beamed with excitement as she hugged her and Brayden.

"Congrats, bro." Ben grinned. "Welcome to the family, Delilah."

"I couldn't be happier for the both of you." I held up my glass of bourbon. "Congratulations."

"There's something else," Brayden said. "Delilah is pregnant. We're having a baby."

After the boys helped clean up and left, Stella and I went upstairs and got ready for bed.

"We're going to be grandparents, Miles," Stella said.

"I can't believe it, sweetheart."

"Two weddings and a baby." She climbed into bed and laid her head on my chest.

"We did good, don't you think?" I kissed the top of her head. "We raised two wonderful and respectful boys who found the love of their lives and are starting their own families. I think we deserve a trip."

"We were just in Italy for our anniversary a couple of months ago." She laughed.

"We deserve another one. Block out some time from your practice because I'm taking you to the Maldives."

"Can we get one of those over-the-water bungalows?" She lifted her head and stared at me.

"Yes. You know I'll give you anything you want." I stroked her cheek. "I love you, Stella."

"I love you too, Miles." She climbed on top of me, grabbed my arms, and held them over my head. "And I'm going to show you just how much." Her lips met mine.

"Damn, I love when you take control." I smiled.

Thank you for reading Baby Drama II. I hope you enjoyed it!

Be sure to check out "More Sizzling Romance" for my other romance novels.

I invite you to join my Sandi's Romance Readers Facebook Group, where we talk about books, romance, and more! Join the fun!

Newsletter
Website
Facebook
Instagram
FOLLOW ME ON AMAZON
TikTok
Bookbub
Goodreads

MORE SIZZLING ROMANCE

Looking for more romance reads about billionaires, second chances, and sports? Check out my other romance novels and escape to another world and from the daily grind of life – one book at a time.

Series:

Forever Series:
Forever Black (Forever, Book 1)
Forever You (Forever, Book 2)
Forever Us (Forever, Book 3)
Being Julia (Forever, Book 4)
Collin (Forever, Book 5)
A Forever Family (Forever, Book 6)
A Forever Christmas (Holiday short story)

Wyatt Brothers Series:

Love, Lust & A Millionaire (Wyatt Brothers, Book 1)
Love, Lust & Liam (Wyatt Brothers, Book 2)

A Millionaire's Love Series:
Lie Next to Me (A Millionaire's Love, Book 1)
When I Lie with You (A Millionaire's Love, Book 2)

Happened Series:
Then You Happened (Happened Series, Book 1)
Then We Happened (Happened Series, Book 2)

Redemption Series:
Carter Grayson (Redemption Series, Book 1)
Chase Calloway (Redemption Series, Book 2)
Jamieson Finn (Redemption Series, Book 3)
Damien Prescott (Redemption Series, Book 4)

Interview Series:
The Interview: New York & Los Angeles Part 1
The Interview: New York & Los Angeles Part 2

Love Series:
Love In Between (Love Series, Book 1)
The Upside of Love (Love Series, Book 2)

Wolfe Brothers Series:
Elijah Wolfe (Wolfe Brothers, Book 1)

Nathan Wolfe (Wolfe Brothers, Book 2)
Mason Wolfe (Wolfe Brothers, Book 3)

Kind Brothers Series:
One of a Kind (Kind Brothers Series, Book 1)
Two of a Kind (Kind Brothers Series, Book 2)
Three of a Kind (Kind Brothers Series, Book 3)
Four of a Kind (Kind Brothers Series, Book 4)
Five of a Kind (Kind Brothers Series, Book 5)
The Kind Brothers (Kind Brothers Series, Book 6)
Six of a Kind (Kind Brothers Series, Book 7)
Seven of a Kind (Kind Brothers Series, Book 8)
Eight of a Kind (Kind Brothers Series, Book 9)
Nine of a Kind (Kind Brothers Series, Book 10)
A Kind Wedding: Jackson & Georgia (Kind Brothers Series, Book 11)
A Kind Wedding: Conner & Charlotte (Kind Brothers Series, Book 12)
A Kind Wedding: Nathan & Sofia (Kind Brothers Series, Book 13)
A Kind Wedding: Christian & Charleigh (Kind Brothers Series, Book 14)
Ten of a Kind (Kind Brothers Series, Book 15)
Eleven of a Kind (Kind Brothers Series, Book 16)
Twelve of a Kind (Kind Brothers Series, Book 17)
Thirteen of a Kind (Kind Brothers Series, Book 18)
Fourteen of a Kind (Kind Brothers Series, Book 19)

One Night Series:
One Night In London
One Night In Paris

MORE SIZZLING ROMANCE

Broken Hearts Series:
Unspoken
A Beautiful Sight

Baby Drama Series:
Baby Drama
Baby Drama II

Standalone Books

The Billionaire's Christmas Baby
His Proposed Deal
The Secret He Holds
The Seduction of Alex Parker
Something About Lorelei
The Exception
Corporate Assets
The Negotiation
Defense
The Con Artist
#Delete
Behind His Lies
Perfectly You
The Escort
The Ring
The Donor
Rewind
Remembering You
When I'm With You
LOGAN (A Hockey Romance)
The Merger
The Property Brokers

Printed in Great Britain
by Amazon